A MURDER AT
RANCHO MANANA

SHERRY KENNEY

A MURDER AT RANCHO MANANA

A NOVEL

Hester Press
Denver, Colorado

A Murder at Rancho Manana
Copyright © 2026 by Sherry Kenney

Published by:

Hester Press
Denver, Colorado
Inquiries: HesterPressCo@gmail.com

Paperback ISBN: 979-8-9868615-2-4
Library of Congress Control Number: 2025922562

Book design: Journey Bound Publishing
Back cover photo: Gabrielle Col

10 9 8 7 6 5 4 3 2 1
First Edition

For Andy

A Murder at
Rancho Manana

The digital clock on June's hotel nightstand read four o'clock A.M. She punched the code she had programmed into her phone for what seemed like the fiftieth time, and again her daughter's recorded voice assured her she would call back as soon as possible. Nothing had changed, other than her rising panic, and the increased self-loathing she felt at her own stupidity. What was she thinking ten hours ago, when she allowed Savannah to drive away with the young woman they had both met just sixty minutes earlier? Couldn't she have thought to ask for Marta's phone number? Then, at least, she would have an area code, a billing address, a bread crumb. Why hadn't she taken a quick photo of the license plate on the older model, rust-dented, red Corolla sedan? What would security at The Boulders think of her as a parent if law enforcement officers asked for footage of her daughter entering the car? Would it come to that? What would her former husband do if she was forced tell him that—this time—she really had lost the baby?

PART ONE

One

Arizona summers were getting longer and warmer, with a record one hundred and seventeen degrees recorded in Phoenix on September 28, 2024. Even a month later, the only way to escape the heat was to stay inside, or to drive in an air-conditioned car from one air-conditioned building to another. Still, with gradually cooling nighttime temps, a pool could feel refreshing. So no one took particular notice of the man reclining on a towel-draped chaise lounge, in the middle of the afternoon, under the shade of an umbrella at Rancho Manana Golf Club, a resort that had once been a dude ranch in the popular tourist destination town of Cave Creek.

Tiffany Layton guided her prospects around the pool area and back through the registration office, having given them a tour of one of the two-bedroom units in the resort-property-turned-timeshare. She invited the couple, a physician and his wife who had come down from North Dakota, to sit with her on the patio at the Tonto Grill and let her answer any questions they might have about interval vacation ownership, and the terms of the contract.

"The best thing about this program is that it really does force you to take a vacation, rather than procrastinating. Although you *can* carry your points forward, it's best to use them currently, and you can even borrow points from the next calendar year. And of course, although this would be your home property, and whichever week you choose would be your home week—meaning that a unit here will always be available to you at that time—you also have access to many other resort properties, based on availability. Even though you own your property, you don't have to maintain it. Everything is handled for you, so you can just show up, relax, and enjoy."

As she proceeded to check off the salient points from her sales script, which she could recite in her sleep, Tiffany glanced periodically toward the pool. The man on the lounge chair had not shifted.

Her prospects were easily convinced, so she led them back to the registration building and into her small private office, where she guided them through a mountain of paperwork, congratulated them on their wise decision to buy not one week but two, and insisted that the engraved luxury ballpoint pens they were signing their names with were a gift from the company.

"You won't regret choosing to purchase here," she assured them, "and your children and grandchildren will thank you."

Tiffany walked her buyers out of the building. It was now after four o'clock; she had been with the couple for almost three hours.

"I'm going to walk back over to the pool and make sure that man hasn't succumbed to heat stroke," Tiffany muttered to herself. She entered the pool area, now being enjoyed by several other guests, through the gate next to the registration office. Two young boys were having a squirt gun fight in the pool. One of them accidentally shot her and mumbled an apology. She continued toward the chaise where the motionless figure still rested, ball cap pulled low over sunglasses, newspaper open to the daily crossword puzzle across his lap, mechanical pencil—she now noticed—on the ground, next to a limp, dangling hand.

"Sir?"

When there was no response, she tentatively touched the man's arm. Although the late afternoon temperature was in the eighties, his skin was cool.

Two

"**HOW** long has he been dead?" Deputy sheriff Jack Powell made his way through the pool area, where his colleague, deputy Trevor Smith, stood watch over the body, now loosely covered with a white hotel sheet.

"Not sure," Smith said. "At least two hours, according to a preliminary statement from the witness who reported him. I mean, what she said was that he hadn't *moved* for two hours. We'll rely on the coroner to figure it out—that, and the cause of death. No sign of foul play. Probably a heart attack. He's a bit overweight."

"What's his name?"

"Bradley Hamilton. Lives in Reno, according to the ID he showed when he checked in. Works for a financial advisory firm—worked, that is. Got into trouble and did some time in prison, lost his licenses, wife divorced him. I just got this off the internet, so we'll take it with a grain of salt for now."

"Anyone here with him?"

"Apparently not. He checked in alone yesterday, for three nights. The second bedroom suite in his unit hasn't been touched. Only one piece of luggage, a medium-sized canvas duffle, and his golf bag—a really old one—which he checked at the pro shop. He's signed up as a single for a round at six-thirty tomorrow morning. Golf shirts, toiletries, laptop. No items particular to a female companion in sight. Strange, coming to a nice place like this without anyone to share the experience with."

"This is one of those timeshare deals now, right? Is Hamilton an owner, or did he agree to sit through a sales pitch in exchange for a package? I think that's how it works."

"Neither. Sometimes the resort still opens to the public, if they have inventory."

"I see. Where's Tony?"

"Looking around the grounds. Ambulance should be here any minute, and then we're off. Thought we might grab a beer at The Horny Toad. Best fried chicken in the state. Wanna' come?"

Three

FRANK Chavez pulled up to the town hall building in Fountain Hills, where the Maricopa County Sheriff's Office was located. He was the ranking deputy for District Seven, where he worked hard to earn the admiration of his professional colleagues and the respect of the citizens of this certified dark sky community, complete with a man-made lake at its center. The lake featured what was once the world's highest fountain. Even though it had lost that distinction over the years, it still faithfully erupted, every hour, on the hour.

"Good morning, Martha." Frank tipped his hat to the receptionist, who had been with the department for as long as he had, and made his way back to his office, where he lowered his six-foot frame into his desk chair and began to multi-task, shuffling through papers in his inbox while listening to voice mail, and booting up his computer for email.

"It's me," said his sister's voice over the speaker. "I didn't want to bother you on your mobile this early. Call me when you can. It's June, again. I don't understand how a woman as smart as she is can get into as much trouble as she does, but this time it's pretty serious."

Frank picked up his cell phone, pulled up his sister's number, and hit the call button. *"Buenos días, mi hermana, qué tal?"*

"It's June. Her daughter, actually. Savannah's a junior at Duke, as sweet and pretty as her mother. I met her yesterday; she flew in from Raleigh-Durham and took an Uber to the clinic. June had booked the two of them a casita at The Boulders—a big splurge on a nurse's budget, but she thought it would be fun. Savannah connected with a friend she had met online, a girl from Mexico who's a student at ASU. They were going to hang out at The Spotted Donkey for the evening, while June got a massage at the spa. The friend was supposed to drop Savannah at the hotel—the cantina closes at ten—and drive back to Tempe. Only, that didn't happen. Savannah hasn't returned and isn't answering her phone. And the only thing June knows about her daughter's new friend is her first name."

Four

"HAVE you gotten the Rancho Manana tox report yet?" Jack Powell asked, as he paused by Trevor Smith's desk on his way to the coffee maker in the kitchenette at the end of the hall.

"Still waiting on it," Trevor said. "But Tony thought he overheard one of the EMTs pointing out a needle mark on Hamilton's right thigh when they put him on the gurney. May or may not mean anything. You missed a good happy hour last night. Although, if I had your lady to go home to, I wouldn't spend time hanging out in bars either. When are you planning on making an honest woman of her?"

"You think it's up to me? I've asked her to marry me a hundred times."

"And?"

"She's not sure she wants to get hitched to a cop. Says she couldn't handle it if I got shot. I keep telling her I can get shot whether we're married or not, but that the odds are against it, either way."

Deputy Tony Block stepped around the corner, a sheet of paper in his hand. "Hot off the printer," he said, handing the page to Trevor. Turning to Jack he asked, "How's Cindy? I swear to God, you're the luckiest son of a gun on the planet. I have no idea why she chose you." He gave his colleague a playful punch on the arm.

"'Cause she's got brains to go with her beauty," Jack said, returning the punch.

"Okay, you two, listen up. Bradley Hamilton died from an injection of sodium chloride." Trevor laid the report Tony had given him on his desk, facing the other deputies. "How do you suppose that happened to him, lying there by the pool at Rancho Manana? Who gave him the shot? Answering those questions, gentlemen, is your mission, should you choose to accept it. And I strongly suggest you do, if you want to keep your jobs.

"The name of the sales agent who first noticed the body is Tiffany Layton," Trevor continued. "One of you get the hell back over to Rancho Manana with forensics, and the other start looking at flights to Reno. I'll get some expert help breaking into Hamilton's devices—both his phone and his laptop are password protected."

Five

FRANK Chavez knocked quietly on the door of the casita. June Lambreth practically fell into his arms when she opened it, to his surprise and discomfort. Her body was wracked with sobs. Frank, always chivalrous but steeped in professionalism, discreetly disengaged from her embrace.

"June, I know how upsetting this situation must be for you. I'm here to help. Why don't we go down to the café in the lobby, and you can tell me everything that's happened." The last thing he wanted was to continue this meeting, with a woman in distress, in her hotel room.

When they were seated at a booth in the corner of the Palo Verde, a casual but sophisticated restaurant that looked out over one of The Boulders' iconic golf courses, two cups of coffee between them, June began to share the events of the previous evening in her genteel southern drawl. This was obviously both painful, and embarrassing, for her.

"My daughter is here over her fall break. She's my—our—only child. My husband and I separated, then divorced, seven years ago. I thought it would be fun for Savannah and me to stay at a resort property, rather than in my efficiency apartment—that's why I booked here. This place has the spa, good restaurants, great views…you know, Frank, we have limited time to create special memories with our daughters."

Frank did know. His twins, Scottie and Ginny, were now thirteen going on thirty, and he and his wife, Margaret, told each other often that the time seemed to be slipping through their fingers.

"Four years ago, Savannah met a young woman from Guadalajara named Marta, in an online support group for daughters of abusive fathers. Let me be clear, my husband was not always a mean person—I would never have married him if he were. But he suffered multiple head injuries and, long story short, over time, they affected his level of patience with the people he loved the most. It was very sad, but at a point in time, I decided my daughter and I would be better off living on our own. Then, when she went away to college, I made a clean break and moved to Arizona."

Frank recalled meeting June on the Fourth of July, in Fountain Hills, three summers ago. She had just come to work at the Scottsdale Mayo Clinic, where his sister, Maria, was nurse supervisor in the cardiac unit. "I remember the first time I met you," he said, "right after you moved. You brought those delicious little pecan pies to our family's picnic."

"Yes, my tassies." His compliment brought a fleeting smile to her full lips, showing off her perfectly white, movie star teeth. Even with no make-up other than a hint of gloss, and with eyes red from crying, Frank thought June was one of the most beautiful women he had ever seen. As his sister had pointed out that very morning, she did have a penchant for getting herself into fixes. But to Frank, that vulnerability just made her more attractive.

"Anyway," June continued, "the online group disbanded, but Savannah and Marta stayed in touch. When my daughter decided to come out for fall break—this is just her second time to visit me here—and realized how close her friend was over in Tempe, it was only natural for the two of them to get together."

June passed a hand over her eyes, and pulled in a deep breath, before continuing.

"We met Marta last night in the lounge, for an hour. The girls were drinking sodas; I had a glass of wine. Then Marta excused herself and went to get her car, which she pulled around in front for Savannah. I kissed my daughter goodbye and waved the girls off without a thought—silly me—then headed to the spa. Supposedly, they were driving over to the Mexican restaurant. I mean, they could have walked…

"I never asked Marta her last name. I'm sure it's in Savannah's contacts, but of course, she has her phone. When she didn't come back to our room last night, I called her. That was about ten-thirty. She said they had decided to go to a club not far away, in Scottsdale, and that she would be back soon, by midnight. She said she hadn't called because she assumed I was already asleep, and she didn't want to wake me. They had met up with some of Marta's friends, she said, and were having a great time. She assured me they weren't drinking much, and just beer. I mean, they *are* twenty-one." Now June sounded defensive.

"Then it got to be midnight, then one, then two…"

"Have you spoken to anyone in security here at the resort? Or to the local authorities?" Frank already knew the answer to his questions.

"What would I say to them, Frank? I feel so negligent. I knew Maria would be at work at six, so I texted her then, and she called me right away. She said you would know what to do. Thank you for coming over. I wish you weren't always having to see me making a mess of my life."

It was all Frank could do to resist covering June's small hands reassuringly with his own.

Six

FRANK walked into the District Four office, which provided contract law enforcement to both Cave Creek and Carefree, and asked for Deputy Smith. Trevor overheard him from his office and came out to greet his former classmate and old friend. "What are you doing here in my territory?" he joked. "Go back to District Seven, where you belong."

"I'd like very much to do that," Frank said. "I'm just over here visiting a friend with a problem. Let me give you the details, and I'll be on my way." He proceeded to summarize his conversation with June.

"So, your friend June's adult daughter has been missing for, what should we say, ten hours?" Trevor raised his eyebrows. "That's assuming we use midnight as our starting point. You know these situations typically resolve themselves, Frank, and I'm a little short staffed right now. But I get it. I'll send someone over to The Boulders to take a report. I mean, it's just around the corner. In the meantime, remind your friend to keep her phone charged and the ringer on."

"So, not to be nosy, but what's going on that has your people tied up?"

"A guy from Reno, who died over at Rancho Manana. At first it looked like natural causes, but after reviewing the coroner's report, we suspect it's murder."

"A murder…at Rancho Manana."

"That's right, Frank. Why the funny look on your face?"

Frank shook his head. "Just thinking, that's all. Sorry. Hey, listen, I really appreciate your help with June. Let me know if there's anything I can do to reciprocate."

Seven

"**HEY** babe, how's your day going?"

"It's fine, busy," said Margaret Chavez. "I'm heading out in a minute to volunteer at La Casita for a couple of hours, then I'm stopping at Harrington House to sign up for a workshop next week. It's on how to communicate with teenagers—not that I need it," she added, with a laugh. "Then, the girls have a soccer game after school. Any chance you can come, Frank?"

"Barring anything unforeseen, I'll be there. The reason I'm calling, other than to hear your sexy voice, is to find out if our copy of Nancy Scott's book is at home. I know it's been on loan to various friends."

"Not only is it here, but it's my book club selection this month. Next Thursday night, in fact. Nancy's coming over to talk about it, and to have dinner with us. That might be a good time for you to take *tu madre* and the girls out for dinner and a movie."

"Sounds good, I'll make a plan. Love you, babe."

"Love you, too."

Eight

"So, who drew the short straw?" Trevor Smith was sitting in the kitchenette at the Division Four office, eating a tuna sandwich and drinking a can of root beer.

"If you mean who has to fly to Reno," Tony said, taking a frozen pot pie out of the microwave, "I guess I did, leaving at four today and picking up a car when I arrive. But hey, it's the closest thing I've had to a vacation in months, so I'll take it. Anyway, Jack didn't want to leave his girlfriend home alone." Tony grinned. "I don't blame him."

"Where do you plan to start?"

"Hamilton lived in an apartment complex near the medical school—University of Nevada. Appears to be quiet, not a swinging singles kind of place. Reno police department arranged for a warrant. We'll look around the unit and interview the neighbors, rule out anything obvious.

"I think the best bet is going to be talking to some of the folks Hamilton scammed—seems likely someone was still holding a grudge. They're spread out over a pretty big area, mainly farmers and ranchers, but some professionals, too. I'm meeting with his parole officer in the morning. Maybe Hamilton mentioned something, or someone, to him."

"Good luck. Keep in touch and let us know what you need. Jack came up empty-handed over at Rancho Manana."

"Thanks, will do."

Nine

JUNE answered a knock at the casita door at five minutes past noon. Her daughter stood before her, an expression of deep remorse on her face.

"I'm so sorry, Momma, please forgive me. I know you've been worried sick."

June began crying and hugging her daughter as close as she could. "You'll never know, Savannah, that is, until you have your own little girl." Then she held her daughter at arm's length and looked her over from head to toe. Savannah, still wearing the clothes she had worn the day before, did not appear to be harmed in any way. "Where have you been, darling? Why didn't you call me?"

"I'm so sorry, Momma, really, I am. I know how thoughtless I've been, and I'll make it up to you, I promise. I won't leave your side for the next two days.

"Marta and I hung out at the cantina until it closed, then we went to a bar in Scottsdale. That's when you called me. When that bar closed at midnight, we decided to go over to Tempe, so she could show me where she lives—it's a co-housing community, a really cool place. I was going to call you, even if it meant waking you up, to let you know I planned to spend the night with her, but then I realized I didn't have my phone. I couldn't call you from Marta's phone, because I don't have your new number memorized. We searched her car, and when my phone wasn't there, I realized I must have left it at the bar.

"Sure enough, that's where we found it, just now—the place didn't open until eleven-thirty, but they had it at the hostess desk. It was out of juice, so I still couldn't call. Marta dropped me off here and headed back to Tempe. I'm so sorry."

June had indeed been advised to change her mobile number some months ago, after her phone had been compromised. While having a drink in a bar with a man she had met through an online dating website, she had accessed the password manager on her phone to order a book he'd suggested. Then, when she excused herself to go to the restroom, he asked to look at her photos. It wasn't until the next day that she realized he had gone to her payment app and sent himself five thousand dollars. The only reason she had that much money in her account in the first place is that her paycheck had just been deposited. Which, in hindsight, he probably knew. On that occasion, too, she had gone to Maria, crying and cringing with embarrassment at her own stupidity. Maria had told Frank, who helped June file a fraud report and a description of the thief. But, as she'd found out the hard way, the people who did this kind of thing were skillful, and difficult to catch.

"Don't cry, darling," June said, taking a deep breath. "I just need to send a couple of texts and let people know you're okay. Then let's put this behind us and get some lunch. Why don't you splash some water on your face and change into some fresh clothes. And Savannah, promise me you'll never leave your phone in a bar again."

Ten

Deputy Tony Block landed at Reno-Tahoe International Airport, and made his way to the rental car counter to sign an agreement and pick up his keys. He had reserved a mid-size sedan for three days, secretly hoping not to need it for that long. He found the car, threw his overnight bag into the back seat, and input Bradley Hamilton's address into the vehicle's GPS. Sergeant Mike Milligan, with the Reno police, was waiting for him there with a warrant.

The two men greeted each other, then used the key Milligan had obtained from the property manager to enter Hamilton's home. Tony flipped the light switch next to the door, and they looked around. The place was non-descript—brown shag carpet, beige walls, thrift store furniture—no frills. They entered the bedroom, where just a few shirts and pairs of pants hung in the closet. A pair of newer tennis shoes, and a pair of worn, leather work boots, stood in the corner.

"Refresh my memory about when this guy got out of prison?" Milligan said. "He certainly hasn't done much shopping since then."

"Three months ago," Tony said. He poked around the bedroom, opening drawers that held a few pairs of socks and underwear, and a couple of tee shirts. He opened the medicine cabinet in the bathroom, which was empty. He followed Milligan back through the living room and into the kitchen, where a map of Arizona was spread out on a small kitchen table, an empty coffee cup sitting on it.

"He was definitely a minimalist," Milligan said, opening the refrigerator and freezer doors, revealing a couple of Miller Lites and a frozen Salisbury steak dinner. A banana was turning brown next to a coffee maker with a half-filled pot. A used cereal bowl sat in the sink.

"No photos, no books, no business cards, no slips of paper with interesting tidbits of information—not much at all, I'm afraid. Let's go have a beer. I assume someone with a name like Milligan knows where to find a good pub."

Eleven

TONY slept fitfully. His night was filled with disconcerting dreams. The complimentary rubber eggs and fruit cocktail at the hotel's breakfast buffet filled him up before he walked across the street to the Nevada Division of Parole and Probation.

"Deputy Tony Block to see Officer Koenig," he told the receptionist.

"He'll be right with you, Deputy Block. He's on a phone call. Would you like a cup of coffee while you wait?"

"Yes, please. Black, with two sugars."

The receptionist returned with the coffee, and led Tony into a small interview room, where he sat with his thoughts until a large, congenial man entered and introduced himself. Tony rose to shake his hand and knew immediately that Tim Koenig was successful at his job—at least, as successful as possible when working with folks who have the odds stacked against them.

"So, Deputy Block," Koenig dove in, "I understand you're investigating the murder of Brad Hamilton."

"That's right," said Tony. "Do you know anyone who wanted him dead?"

Koenig smiled ruefully. "Any one of a number of people whose lives he ruined, I imagine. The simpler question is, who didn't want him dead? In hindsight, the governor should probably have never given him clemency. He was safer in prison. But he was a model inmate, and his punishment was deemed to have been too harsh. So, well, you know what happened. That's why you're here. I'd like to help you if I can."

"Did Hamilton ever mention any of his victims to you, anyone who had contacted him or threatened him since he got out of the pen?"

"Not specifically. But he was wary. He moved here hoping to live quietly, in a place where he wasn't known. But these days, with the internet and all, it's hard to be anonymous. He mentioned a couple of times that he thought he was being watched. I told him to go to the police, if he was really worried, but I don't think he ever did. And he had to work—I mean, he paid out everything he had in restitution. So, no savings, no retirement funds. It was tough. He was a smart man. Too bad he chose to misuse his talent."

"What landed him in jail, exactly?"

"It's complicated; not sure I understand it myself. Let's just say he robbed Peter to pay Paul."

"Ponzi?"

"Something like that. You'll probably want to start by getting in touch with some of the folks who testified at his trial. But I gotta warn you, there's a lot of pain out there."

"Assuming you can help me get a transcript from the trial?" Tony asked, realizing, at that moment, that he would not be turning the rental car in early.

Twelve

FRANK Chavez slipped into his house through the back door and headed quietly down the hall to his bedroom. He tiptoed, trying not to wake his mother, who was asleep in her chair in the living room, one of her favorite sitcoms playing at a low volume. He hoped to pick up the book he had called his wife about and exit undetected. He located it, *A Murder at Rancho Manana*, on Margaret's bedside table, and started back down the hall.

"*Francisco? Francisco, eres tú?*" Aurelia asked, dreamily.

"*Si, Mamá, soy yo.*" He crossed the room and kissed the top of her head. "*Tengo que volver a trabajar ahora. Necesitas algo?*" he asked, offering to bring anything she needed before he left again.

"*No, estoy bien. Te quiero.*"

"*Y tú también, Mamá. Adiós, hasta luego.*" Frank kissed his mother a second time and headed for the back door, grabbing a soda from the refrigerator as he passed.

Thirteen

"**FRANK** Chavez, long time no see! To what do I owe the honor?" Nancy Scott's ebullient voice bubbled through the speakerphone on his desk. Frank could visualize his friend over in Tonto Verde, with her red, slightly wild hair, and her grinning, freckled face. Almost two years ago he had engaged her assistance in solving a mystery—a prominent doctor found dead in his hot tub—and proving her friends John and Jennifer Crouch innocent of any crime.

"How've you been, Nancy? It's a dubious honor, I'm afraid. There's been a murder over at Rancho Manana, and, well, normally that's such a quiet place that it made me think of your book, and whether there might be some connection."

"Wow, you mean, like a copycat killing or something?"

"Maybe. It's District Four's case; the guy in charge there is a friend of mine. I haven't said anything to him. Thought I'd talk to you first."

"Wow, Frank, I've been wishing we could collaborate on something. I need some fresh ideas for the new book I'm working on. How can I help?"

"Why don't I check in with Deputy Smith—that's my buddy—and find out what they have at this point. If it seems relevant, I'll tell him about you and your book and facilitate an introduction. I wanted to give you a heads-up first. Oh, and I understand you're attending Margaret's book club meeting next week at our house. I'll be out with Mom and the girls, so I'll miss you. Anyway, I'm glad you're doing well. I may be back in touch."

"Sounds good, Frank. Thanks for calling!"

Fourteen

"**HEY** Tony, making any progress up there in Reno?"

"Not much, yet, but I'll tell you what I know so far. Brad Hamilton was one successful dude, or at least he appeared to be. Sold insurance, retirement plans, investments of all kinds—oil and gas, real estate limited partnerships, you name it, he sold it. The best I can understand—and I gotta tell you, I'm way out of my league on this—he'd take money from a client, make a small deposit on their behalf to the company whose product he'd sold 'em, take a big advance from the company, give enough of the money back to the client to make 'em think they'd hit a home run, and then repeat it with the next client. And these are good, hard-working people—farmers and ranchers, business owners, doctors…

"Meanwhile, Hamilton's pocketing most of the money, living the high life in Vegas. Mansion, with a pool and a putting green. Giving his gorgeous wife jewelry and anything else she wants, including the funds to sponsor the society bashes she helps put on, sending his two kids to private schools, flying the family to Park City and Aspen to ski…"

"Geez," said Trevor. "But he got caught."

"He did, and it all came tumbling down. A jury found him guilty of securities fraud and felony theft, and the judge sentenced him to five years for each one of the victims represented in the case—over a hundred years behind bars. Originally, they sent him to Nevada State Prison. He was there for eight years, but that place closed in 2012. Hamilton had been exemplary, so they relocated him to Carlin Conservation Camp, minimum security."

"And?"

"And he started teaching the other inmates financial skills— basic stuff like budgeting, and balancing a checkbook, and how compound interest works. Things they could use to get ahead, honestly, on the outside. He gave motivational talks about how crime never pays in the long run, and the importance of not betraying people's trust. Somehow, the governor got wind of it and decided to make Hamilton a poster child for the rewards of good behavior. That, plus the punishment seemed a bit harsh to begin with. Hamilton walked out after serving twenty years of his sentence, a free, albeit broke, man. Nothing in his apartment lent a clue to what's been going on in his life, or what took him to Arizona, although he had been looking at a map of the state. Any luck getting into his electronics?"

"Jack and I are meeting with a team from IT in a bit; hopefully they'll have something for us. I'm assuming we won't be seeing you for a while."

"Nope, you won't. I cancelled my flight home—taking a road trip instead, Reno to Vegas. Stopping along the way to visit some of Hamilton's clients. I'm focusing on the ones who testified."

"Be careful—a lot of crazies on the road."

"Will do. Later."

Fifteen

"**Trevor?** Frank here. Thanks again for sending someone over to talk to my friend June. Thank God the girl turned up."

"No problem. Any time. What's happening?"

"It's about the murder you're investigating. Any more information about the victim?"

"A little. Financial type. Got greedy with his clients, stole from 'em, ended up spending time in the pen. Got out for good behavior, but that didn't do anything for his victims. Working theory is that one of them wanted revenge. One of our men is making his way down from Reno, meeting up with some of 'em. You got any other ideas, mister overachiever-straight-A-student?"

Frank laughed. "You just can't get over my beating you out of that number one spot at the academy, can you? I keep telling you, runner-up ain't bad. The fact is, I may have a thread for you. You can pull it or not. There's a writer out in Tonto Verde, name's Nancy Scott. She's a terrific gal. Her genre is mystery, and about eighteen months ago she published a book with the title *A Murder at Rancho Manana*. Her victim sold financial products. I told her you might decide to give her a call."

"Hmmm. Can't hurt. What's her number?"

Sixteen

"**HEY,** babe." Frank sat down next to his wife on her stadium blanket in the bleachers at Fountain Hills High School. "How're we doing?"

"We're doing great!" She lowered her voice. "Scottie's had two goals, and Ginny's blocked two. I know I'm not objective, but these girls of ours are pretty awesome."

"Just like their mother." He put his arm around her and pulled her close, nuzzling her hair with his nose.

"Frank, PDA." She laughed softly. "Someone in the public eye needs to protect his reputation."

"I know, and I've been thinking. Maybe we should get out of town. Not too far out, just over to Cave Creek. Are you up for a date night? I'll take you to the Tonto Grill later, assuming I can get us a reservation."

"A date night, what's that?" She laughed. "I'm teasing. It sounds lovely. I can pick up a pizza for Mom and the girls on the way home from soccer. They have homework."

"Perfect." They looked back at the field just in time to see Scottie—older than her twin sister by fifteen minutes—score her third goal.

"Go, Falcons!" they cheered in unison.

Seventeen

TONY pulled up in front of a farmhouse that sat at the end of a winding road a mile off Interstate 95. A large dog of indeterminate breed pulled itself up from a shady spot next to the front porch that ran the length of the house and limped toward him. He barked loudly at first, then attempted to lick him to death. Tony held his hand palm down to be sniffed and approved, then petted the long brown fur of the animal's head and neck, scratching its ears and murmuring "good boy".

A tall, trim woman, wearing jeans and a light pink western style shirt, came around the corner of the house, removing gardening gloves as she walked. "You must be Deputy Block. I see you've met Homer," she laughed, extending her hand in greeting. "I'm Sallie Macomber. Come inside, and I'll get you something cool to drink."

She held the front door of the house open for Tony to pass through, and motioned toward a large, oak dining room table, where he stood next to one of the chairs, waiting for Sallie to sit first. She poured tea into a glass of ice with a lemon slice wedged between the cubes and handed it to Tony. "Sugar?" she asked, indicating the bowl on the table.

"Thank you, ma'am," he said, adding a big spoonful. "I appreciate you letting me stop by."

"Of course. Did I understand you to say that you're investigating Brad Hamilton's death?"

"That's right, ma'am. We think he may have been murdered. Do you have any idea who might have done it?"

"Well, I can certainly imagine there are people out there who think he got off too easy, if that's what you mean. The amount of damage he did…there are some people whose lives he ruined."

"Would you place yourself in that category?" Tony asked the question with as much sensitivity as he could.

"Yes and no," said Sallie. "My husband and I turned over our life savings to Brad. It's hard to realize it now, but he was a man we instinctively trusted. He told us he was going to invest it for our retirement, not that farmers ever really retire. But we *had* thought about selling this place someday, and Brad had some creative ideas about turning it over to our children, should they be interested in continuing it.

"Anyway, we lost everything. I'm sure you know something about Brad's methods. Then, my husband was diagnosed with colon cancer. The doctors wouldn't say for sure that there was any connection, but apparently extreme stress can lower one's immune system and make it harder to fight off disease. John died the day before our thirtieth wedding anniversary. Fortunately, the kids were all educated by then, but I had nothing, and a mortgage to pay."

Tony grimaced.

"But Brad had sold my husband a life insurance policy for one and a half million dollars. I wasn't convinced he needed that much, but Brad was a heck of a good salesman. So, unlike most of his victims, money is something I've not had to worry about, at least, not since I lost my husband."

Her voice sounded a little shaky, and Tony thought he detected tears in her eyes. But she lowered her lids and busied herself with the dog, taking his head in her hands and scratching him behind the ears.

Tony rose reluctantly; it was pleasant here at Sallie's table. "I think that's all I need for now. I'm so sorry about your husband, Mrs. Macomber. Thank you again for your time."

Eighteen

ONE *down, God knows how many to go*. Tony was back on Ninety-five now, barreling down the highway toward Tonopah, a town with a compelling origin story, still regarded as "Queen of the Silver Camps", though today it was mainly a tourist destination. Among other things, Tonapah was known for being the site of Howard Hughes' marriage to Jean Peters. The Mizpah Hotel, named after a once-famous silver mine and now on the U. S. National Register of Historic Places, provided the best lodging in town. It had a coffee shop in the lobby, which is where Tony planned to meet Bruce Beneman.

Beneman and his brother, Tom, were cattle ranchers, and had—according to the court documents Tony had read—entrusted Brad Hamilton with the investment of their corporate retirement plan. The Double B Ranch was one of the first in Nevada to raise grass-fed beef, at a time when many consumers were becoming concerned about the hormones and pesticides in their food. The brothers had owned a thriving enterprise, and had planned—again, according to what Tony had read—to branch into other areas in the healthier meat marketplace.

Tony pulled up to the front of the hotel, got out, and stretched his legs, scanning the horizon. The town looked like a set out of the Wyatt Earp television series, complete with hitching post. There was a certain appeal to it; had it been later in the day, Tony might consider staying the night, although he suspected the Mizpah rates were higher than what he could comfortably put on his expense account.

"Deputy Block?"

Tony started, and turned to see the quintessential rugged cowboy standing behind him—weathered skin and grizzled beard, shaggy gray hair beneath his Stetson, worn leather belt holding up faded jeans, and ancient but cared-for boots.

"Mr. Beneman?" Tony accepted the extended hand and shook it. "This is quite some town you have here. Shall we go inside and have something to eat? I take it your brother decided not to join us."

When they were seated, with menus in hand, Beneman answered Tony's question. "Tom's not doing so well these days. Fact is, he hasn't been doing well for years. After the, shall we say, debacle with the money, he took to drinking. Wife eventually left him, kids stopped coming around. He went to rehab, eventually, and at least now he gets to see his grandkids. Mostly, he just sits in his easy chair and watches old movies, game shows, whatever's on. He's my younger brother, mind you. He was the star of the family once upon a time. Got a scholarship to UC, Davis."

A server wearing black pants and white shirt approached the booth where the two men sat. They ordered coffees and BLTs.

"Do you mind telling me what happened, with Brad Hamilton, I mean? We're trying to find his killer. We think whoever it was may have been one of *his* victims. Don't get me wrong; I'm not accusing *you*. Just gathering information."

"I don't like talking about it, as you can imagine, but I guess that's why we're here," said the older man.

"I understand," Tony nodded sympathetically. Any one of these folks could have been justified in wanting to see Hamilton dead.

"Tom and I took over the ranch early on. Dad was one of those great guys who encouraged us to try out new ideas, didn't say things like 'we've never done it that way'. Grass-fed beef was the staple, but we wanted to branch out to lamb, pork, even goat meat. Dad was all for it.

"Hamilton came along and offered to help us get a better return on our retirement funds. Showed us a way to invest the funds back into our business, through an ESOP—that stands for Employee Stock Ownership Plan. The ranch had grown quite large by then. We had a full-time crew of eleven, fourteen hundred cows, and nine thousand yearlings on over five million acres."

"Wow," said Tony.

"Wow is right," said Beneman. "People around here thought we were rich, and we were, although not the kind of rich that city slickers relate to. But that all changed, almost overnight. Hamilton made off with most of our money. *Poof!* It just disappeared. The way it came out at the trial, he used our money to support his own lifestyle, apparently intending to replace it when we needed it, with other people's money. Can you imagine? I mean, the guy seemed trustworthy, and he's obviously smart. Why didn't he just find a way to make an honest living?"

Great question, thought Tony. "So what happened?"

Their food arrived, and they dug in.

"We auctioned off half of the livestock, turned our leases back to the BLM," Beneman said between bites. We let most of the crew go and worked our butts off. Here I am, doing okay. But Tom, like I said…"

"Any idea who might have killed Hamilton?" Tony asked.

"Nah. Could have been anyone, I guess. Not worth the trouble by me." Beneman wiped his mouth with the cloth napkin and signaled for their check.

Nineteen

BACK on ninety-five, Tony spoke into his smartphone, requesting it call Trevor Smith.

"Just checking in," he said, when Trevor picked up.

"How's it going?"

"Not bad. But at this rate, I could be here until next year. So far, the people I've met have every reason to wish Hamilton dead, but they're all too nice to have done it." Tony smiled wryly as he thought about Sallie, and Bruce.

"Sad. Hey, listen, I had a call from your buddy, Milligan, cop in Reno? I guess he tried you first and went directly to voicemail. They're done with Hamilton's apartment—lifted some prints, all belonging to him. Confirmed the beater in his parking space was registered to him. That map you mentioned? This is a small thing, but it's not Triple A, or one you'd get at a state visitor's station. Barnes and Noble sells 'em, and they're not cheap. Hamilton had a charge a couple of months ago that might have been for that map."

"Interesting. Could be he was thinking of moving. Or down for a job interview, maybe? Or visiting a friend, if he still had any. From what I understand, his friends became his clients, which means they became his victims. What'd the IT team come up with?"

"They cracked both devices, but Hamilton was savvy with his security. Everything requires two-step authentication. We're getting subpoenas for his bank account, which is in Vegas, and for his phone records. Emails and texts were scant. No photos. The guy could have been legitimately trying to start a new life, under the radar, but someone begrudged him the opportunity. We need to find that person, although, my hunch is, he or she isn't a threat to anyone else. Where are you staying tonight?"

"Stagecoach Hotel, in Beatty," said Tony.

"Beatty? Never heard of it."

"Two hours north of Vegas, population six hundred. I'm meeting the Allens—Barton and Jessica. Mid- forties, younger than most of Hamilton's clients. Apparently, Jessica's parents died in a car accident and left her a large fortune. Hamilton invested the inheritance for her and turned it into a *small* fortune."

"Sweet Jesus," said Trevor. "Hey, I gotta go. I have a call coming in."

The line went dead.

Twenty

TONY took a corner table in the bar, located in the casino adjacent to the Stagecoach Hotel. He ordered a root beer and closed his strained, dry eyes briefly. When he opened them, he saw Barton and Jessica Allen entering the casino. He wasn't sure how he knew it was them, except perhaps that she looked like East Coast money—old East Coast money. Small designer handbag, understated jewelry, perfect posture. They walked toward him, smiling, as his waitress set a chilled, frothy beverage down at his place. Tony rose to greet the couple, as the waitress lingered. Barton ordered a gin martini, and Jessica asked if the bartender could make an espresso one. The men shook hands, and they all sat.

The faint fragrance of Jessica's perfume wafted toward Tony. He thought it was a scent he had previously experienced—a classic—not that he knew anything about women's perfume. Barton was dressed casually in a golf shirt and khakis, loafers with no socks. Jessica wore a black linen sheath and flat silver sandals. Her shoulder length ash blond hair was parted on one side, no bangs. Her makeup was flawless. Tony assumed they were having dinner somewhere after their interview, though he hadn't seen any place in town classy enough to match her style.

"Thank you for coming in to meet me, Jessica, Barton," he began.

"Call me Bart. We're happy to do it, Deputy Block. There's no need for you to drive all the way out to our place."

Their drinks arrived. "Cheers," said Jessica, lifting her glass and taking a sip. Tony had never heard of an espresso martini, but he intended to try one later.

"So, someone killed Brad Hamilton," said Bart. "We hadn't heard. We don't always read the local papers."

You subscribe to the Wall Street Journal *and* The New York Times, *right?* "I understand," said Tony. "What's your reaction to his death?"

Bart hesitated, seeming to choose his words carefully. "I'm surprised, of course. One never expects the murder of an acquaintance. I'd guess there are quite a few of us who would have preferred he serve out his sentence, which, of course, was life, but to kill him is a different story. I understand he left prison a changed man. Unfortunately, that doesn't reverse the damage he did before he went in."

Tony glanced at Jessica, who appeared to be listening intently. "It was *your* inheritance Hamilton invested, if I read the court documents correctly. That must have been devastating for you— the loss of your parents, and then the loss of their money," he said.

"The loss of my parents, yes, devastating. The loss of their money…yes and no. I was an only child, a privileged child, who grew up in Bridgeport, Connecticut. I went to good schools and made wonderful friends. And then, I married the man of my dreams, who has been very successful in his chosen profession." She smiled at her husband, and continued.

"I have so much to be grateful for. If I were to dwell on my financial loss, I'd be missing out on too much joy—husband, children, friends, Bart's parents and his siblings, our wonderful life. I didn't do anything to deserve that wealth, other than to be born into the right family. And my parents gave me so much more than money. I am truly blessed, Deputy Block."

Is this woman for real? Tony decided to try a different tact. "So, what is your line of work, Bart?"

"I'm a lawyer by training. I grew up in Oregon, studied at Lewis and Clark, graduated and took the bar exam, then applied for a job clear across the country, as general counsel for a pharmaceutical company. Unlike my wife, I did *not* grow up with money. I'm a public-school kid, married up, for sure. In fact, I married the boss's daughter. Her parents took me in and accepted me, unconditionally. Like she said, they were exceptional people.

"After Dad's death—they insisted from the beginning I call them 'Mom' and 'Dad'—I continued with the business until it was sold. By then, I had been promoted to chief legal officer, and we had two children. Jess and I decided to move back west. I'd always wanted to own a ranch, even though I didn't know much about it. We found our place and bought it."

"One of our children has Down Syndrome," Jessica said, "and I got involved with the university's program in Las Vegas. That's how I met Margie Hamilton, Brad's wife. Her sister had a child with Down Syndrome, and she became involved in fundraising for the National Society, chaired a fundraiser for them in Las Vegas, and invited me to get involved. Have you met Margie yet?"

Tony shook his head.

"She's one of the loveliest, most energetic women I've ever known. We met Brad socially, through her. He offered to help with our investments, which at the time were still with a trust company back in New York. We really liked them as a couple. We should have done more due diligence."

Tony saw the couple link hands under the table, saw them exchange a fleeting glance into each other's eyes.

"Bottom line is, we're fine, Deputy. We could be much better off than we are, but we're fine. I'm afraid we have to go now. Please call if we can be of further assistance," Bart said, pushing his chair back and rising.

"Will do, thank you again." Tony stood and shook hands with each of the Allens. Another interview down, but it didn't seem to have gotten him any closer to catching a killer.

Twenty-one

FRANK and Margaret Chavez arrived at the Tonto Grill at Rancho Manana before the sun had set. Frank was driving her car for the sake of anonymity. He pulled into the closest parking space he could find, then walked around to the passenger side to open his wife's door. They greeted the hostess, who led them to a table on the patio that looked out onto the eleventh hole. Frank's schedule didn't allow him to play golf, nor did his budget. But he had played in a charity event once at the Rancho Manana course, and recognized the hole as a short par three that required hitting over a trickle of a creek to an elevated green. He ordered a beer, and Margaret requested the restaurant's signature Mexican Martini. Then they leaned back in their chairs, expelled deep breaths, and gazed into each other's eyes.

"I love you, Margaret," Frank said, finally breaking the silence.

"I love you, too," she responded, smiling at him from across the table.

Their drinks arrived, and Frank toasted their marriage. After ordering an appetizer, they resumed the conversation they'd been having in the car. For the most part, their life together revolved around soccer games and the other activities their girls were involved in, but Frank also wanted to hear about the workshop Margaret had registered to attend at Harrington House, a gathering place that served the interests and needs of the Fountain Hills community.

At one point Frank looked off toward the pool area behind the resort's guest registration office.

"Yes…?" Margaret said, dragging the word out slowly.

"Reading my mind again, are you?" Frank laughed sheepishly. "It's just that, there was a murder here, over there by the pool, just a few days ago. According to my buddy, Trevor, the guy died after an injection of sodium chloride. I'm just trying to figure out how that could have happened, in broad daylight, I mean. I'm sorry, honey."

"No apology necessary. I wondered why you chose this spot to bring me to. Now I understand, and I'm not complaining! Maybe there was some kind of a distraction, you know, so that no one noticed the victim getting jabbed with a syringe."

"Keep going, babe."

"Well, there's certainly no shortage of distractions in the desert! A snake, perhaps, or a tarantula, or a Gila monster? A squadron of javalinas would surely distract, although I don't know how they would get in. I guess someone could have left the gate open…"

Frank laughed at the image of a group of these strange mammals that resembled wild boars prancing around the swimming pool on their cloven hooves. The peccaries, their technical name, had a terrible odor and could be aggressive if startled.

"I am so impressed you know what a group of javalinas is called! I'm with you—no idea how they could have gotten in. But I think you may be on to something. A distraction makes sense."

Their entrées arrived—the Ancho Chili-Rubbed Filet for him, the Tumbleweed Salad with Mexican White Shrimp Skewer for her. The menu at the Tonto Bar and Grill hadn't changed in years; there was no need. Frank knew the restaurant did a thriving lunch and dinner business seven days a week, with tourists and locals alike. The bar was always full of people who had shown up without a reservation, hoping for a no-show, and both the patio and the dining room were in high demand year-round.

Margaret asked for a glass of white wine. Frank stayed with water. He was almost an hour from Fountain Hills, and off duty for the evening, but anything could happen. The words decaled in gold on the SUV which now sat in his driveway at home—Integrity, Accountability & Community—might as well have been engraved on his heart. That's how seriously he took his job.

On the drive back they were quiet, their hands touching lightly. When Frank helped Margaret out of the car, he tipped her chin up and kissed her welcoming lips. "This was fun," he murmured into her ear. "May I call you again?"

She giggled.

"Shhh…," he touched his finger to her lips.

He led her into the house and through the kitchen, past the bedroom where their twin daughters appeared to be sleeping, past Aurelia's bedroom, where his mother snored lightly, and into their own room at the end of the hall. He locked the door, taking care not to make a sound, and in the dark turned to take his wife in his arms. He gently undressed her and removed his own clothes without allowing his lips to separate from hers. Then he picked her up, still kissing her, and carried her to bed.

Twenty-two

TONY was finishing his second espresso martini when an attractive woman with a red mane asked if she could join him. "Please," he said, "be my guest. What are you drinking?"

"I'll have what you're having," she said.

"Great. We may *both* be up all night. My name's Tony."

"I'm Angela."

Tony motioned the waitress over and ordered two drinks, then turned back to his companion. She was older than him, but not by much. She had stories, he was sure of that; he could read them in her tired, but beautiful, green eyes. When their drinks arrived, she asked what he was doing in Beatty.

"Listening to how some really nice people got screwed," he said, conscious he might be slurring his words a bit. "Pardon my French."

"That's sad," said Angela. "People should only get screwed if they want to."

Tony laughed. "I like you, Angela. What are *you* doing in Beatty?"

"Anything I can to make a living—housekeeping, bartending, substitute teaching…"

"You sound like a woman of many talents." He was enjoying this back-and-forth banter with an attractive female, so missing in his life since he lost Lizzy. She was also a redhead, with a temper to go with it, though he knew that stereotype was hogwash.

"Yes, and I haven't listed them all…"

Tony considered his pristine hotel room, just a few steps away. Angela seemed willing. *Should I stay or should I go?*

He stood, as if to stretch his legs. "It's been a pleasure to meet you, Angela. I have an early start in the morning. Please take good care of yourself."

He paid cash at the bar on his way out.

Twenty-three

"**Nancy** Scott speaking."

"Ms. Scott, my name is Trevor Smith. I'm with the Maricopa County sheriff's office, District Four, over in Cave Creek. My colleague, Frank Chavez, in the District Seven office, said you might be able to help me with a case I'm working on."

"Deputy Chavez told me you might be calling, Deputy Smith. I'm happy to help if I can. Frank said you were investigating a murder at Rancho Manana. It's a little eerie, given that's the title of my book. Please call me Nancy."

"Thank you, Nancy, call me Trevor. You're correct, we're investigating a death that appears to have been a murder by lethal injection. Frank wondered if your book, fiction I presume, might provide us with some clue as to who committed our crime."

"My book is definitely fiction! I'll be horrified if you discover that someone copied what I made up! I mean, I would never have imagined in a hundred years…"

Frank had warned Trevor that Nancy was excitable, so he had his most soothing voice at the ready. "Ms. Scott, Nancy, copycat murders sometimes happen. If that's what this is—and I'm not saying it is—you bear no guilt whatsoever. But in your book, the person who was murdered—at Rancho Manana—who was he?"

"I'll be honest, Trevor, I created him, but I got the idea for his character from a man who lived in Colorado, before he went to prison. My husband and I were in Denver; Ben still works there, he's an architect. The person I modeled my character after defrauded a whole lot of people out of a whole lot of money, like Bernie Madoff, only not quite on that scale. But the sentence he got *was* on the same scale. So, at a point in time, the governor of Colorado commuted his sentence. In my book, one of his victims comes after him."

The similarities seemed striking. "So, Nancy, in your book, who commits the murder?" He halfway expected an author's response to be *you'll have to read the book, Trevor.*

"It was a doctor."

"Really? A doctor?"

"Yes. A prominent one. His parents had entrusted their life savings to my victim, and they lost everything. They had a special needs trust for their disabled daughter—gone. They had three homes, two in Colorado and the other in Florida, the second and third—gone. They had significant cash and investments—all gone. They ended up with nothing but monthly Social Security payments, and their primary residence, which they could barely afford to keep up. The son assured his parents he would provide for them, and for his sister, too. But before he could make good on his word, all three died in a suicide pact. They turned on the gas in the basement of their house."

Trevor was speechless. *Sweet Jesus. Had these horrible things really happened?*

Nancy sighed. "Like I said, Trevor, my book is total fiction. My victim is based on a person I read about in the papers, and I embellished the story."

Trevor recovered. "Thank you for your time, Nancy. I intend to read the book. Do you have another one in progress?"

"I do. The working title is *Second to Die*. And thanks in advance for reading my book, Trevor! If you like it, would you please review it?"

Twenty-four

"NANCY, I really liked your book!" said Vicki, one of seven women seated around the table in the Chavez dining room. Margaret had prepared a dinner of taco salad and posole for the six book club members and their guest author, and they were now beginning a second round of margaritas and getting down to their discussion.

"We've been together for ten years," Deb added, "and we mostly read non-fiction, so it's fun to read a mystery, especially one set here in the desert. From what I learned through a little internet research, your victim is loosely based on a real person. What made you choose him, and what made you decide to kill his fictional persona off?"

Nancy smiled.

"I'm glad you asked me that, and, as far as I know, the real guy is alive and kicking." She suddenly flashed back to her conversation with deputy sheriff Trevor Smith, which sent a little shiver through her body. She sipped her drink before continuing, licking a grain of salt from her lip.

"I wanted to illustrate two beliefs I hold in tension. The first, is that even people guilty of terrible acts are capable of transformation, which is why I oppose the death penalty. The second, is that forgiving people for those terrible acts—or sometimes, just unintentional slights!—is the hardest thing we humans are asked to do. Even those of us who preach it as part of our religion!"

The room was quiet, although Nancy thought she detected a nod or two among the group. She waited for the next question, which came from her hostess.

"I was impressed with the way you were able to describe how those who had lost their life savings felt. You made their emotions so real that it brought tears to my eyes. Was it hard to put yourself in their place?"

"In a word, yes. Developing deep point of view is always a challenge for a fiction writer, especially when—thank God!—this kind of loss wasn't anything I'd personally experienced." Nancy thought about her good friend, Jennifer Crouch, who *had* experienced financial loss, though not because anyone betrayed her trust. Her husband, John, had sold off their investments during the recession. They had been broke, but Jennifer had never confronted him. Gradually, he made it all back. The thought of these two warmed her heart. Ben was flying in from Denver in the morning; hopefully, the four of them could get together over the weekend.

The discussion continued until one of the women yawned.

"What time are you expecting Frank and the girls?" Nancy asked Margaret.

"Any time now."

"Well, please say 'hi' to my favorite law enforcement officer. Ladies, it was great meeting you all. Thank you for inviting me tonight! I'd better hop onto McDowell and head back through the park to Tonto Verde."

PART TWO

Twenty-five

JUNE Lambreth sat in the cafeteria of the Mayo Clinic in Scottsdale. She was feeling somewhat bereft, but erased her glum expression when she caught sight of Maria Chavez headed in her direction.

"Hey, girlfriend," June drawled, "come sit down and keep me company. I'm feeling kind of sad since Savannah left."

Maria pulled out the chair next to June's. "It must be hard, having her here after going so long without seeing her, and then having to say 'goodbye'. I take it the visit turned out well after its false start?"

"Extremely well. In fact, we're now planning to spend Christmas together—we're thinking of taking a trip to Mexico…"

"That's awesome, June, congratulations. I need a second cup of coffee; can I get anything for you?" Maria asked.

"No thanks, I need to return to my shift. But I was thinking, maybe we could plan a happy hour sometime soon. How's Frank doing?"

"My brother is amazing, as always. In fact, I'm having dinner with him and Margaret and the girls on Friday. Why don't you come and be my plus one?"

"Are you sure?"

"Absolutely! Margaret always asks about you, and the girls love seeing you too. Six-thirty."

"Thanks, Maria. Please tell Margaret that I'll bring dessert."

Twenty-six

TONY Block left Beatty early, the rising sun blinding him as the highway took a ninety degree turn east toward Indian Springs. He hoped to be in Las Vegas by ten. There, he had an interview with Brad Hamilton's former wife, Margie. As he approached Sin City's limits, his phone rang. *Trevor.*

"What's up?" he answered.

"Just checking in," Trevor said. "Actually, I may have something. I'm thinking our killer might have a medical connection—doctor, nurse maybe. You know, someone who knew how to give our man his deadly shot."

"Don't doctors take some kind of an oath or something?"

"Yeah, Hippocratic, I think it's called. But, you know, if you're planning to kill someone, you're probably not thinking about an oath you took when you graduated from med school."

"Got it. Okay, I'll go back through the transcript with an eye toward that possibility. I mean, doctors make a lot of money—or used to, before the big corporations took 'em over and they became assembly lines. At least that's what I've heard. Hamilton did have some docs as clients."

Trevor grunted his assent.

"So, first order of business is a meeting with Hamilton's ex. Then I'll poke around here looking for formerly rich plastic surgeons and the like. Do you need me to visit Hamilton's bank?"

"Nah," said Trevor. "I talked to someone there yesterday. They'll send his records electronically as soon as I get the subpoena over to 'em this morning. When do you think you'll be home?"

"Tonight, tomorrow at the latest," said Tony. *Who cares?*

"Got it, over and out."

Twenty-seven

TONY pulled up in front of a condominium building on East Tropicana Avenue. He climbed the concrete stairs to the second floor and knocked on the door, its paint peeling around the edges, a peephole a little below his eye level. While he waited, he surveyed the surrounding property. Typical low-budget desert landscaping, nothing requiring water, trees in need of a trim.

The door opened, and a woman he knew from court records to be in her mid-fifties beckoned him in. "Deputy Block? I'm Margie Johnson." He had learned from his research that she had returned to her original name, even though she and her deceased ex had two children surnamed Hamilton.

"It's nice to meet you, Ms. Johnson. Thank you for agreeing to meet with me this morning."

"Of course. Have you learned anything more about who might have killed my former husband?"

She indicated a seat on the sofa. Tony took it, and accepted the cup of coffee she placed on the table in front of him, wishing for a packet of sugar.

"Not anything substantial, I'm afraid. I certainly have talked to some nice folks though, clients of his."

Margie smiled, sadly, it seemed. "Brad worked with some lovely people."

This woman was nothing like what Tony had expected. What *had* he expected, he now wondered. A social dynamo, a gold-digger, a bleached blonde with a boob job?

"How did it all happen?" Tony asked. "I mean, please don't take this wrong, but you seem like an honest person. And according to the people I've spoken with, Hamilton was helpful to them, until he wasn't. So, how did it all go south?"

She sighed. "Neither of us ever intended anyone any harm—at least I never did, and I don't believe Brad did either. We were swept up in the boom after the dot-com bubble burst, and I guess we thought it would go on forever. We bought a big house that someone else had lost to foreclosure, and we quickly got hooked on a lifestyle we couldn't sustain.

"Only, of course, I didn't know any of this in real time. I loved my new-found social status, and Brad supported me in it. He liked seeing my picture in the society pages; he knew how great it was for my ego. He took pride in my wearing the biggest gemstones in the ballroom. Like I said, we were in over our heads, but I didn't know it. Brad was wildly successful by all appearances, and he had to find a workaround."

Tony nodded his head. He almost felt sorry for Margie. *Keeping up with the Joneses, on steroids.* "And his workaround was basically a Ponzi scheme," he said.

"Yes, it was."

"But you didn't know what he was doing?"

"No, I didn't. And the jury agreed."

"Did you suspect?"

Margie glanced at her wristwatch. "Deputy Block," she said, "I hate to be rude, but I need to leave now for an appointment at eleven."

"Of course, Ms. Johnson. Thank you again for your time, and for the coffee."

Twenty-eight

CORNER tables in casino bars were kind of becoming his thing, thought Tony, and it wasn't all bad. Unfortunately, it was too early for an espresso martini. It was also too early to check into a hotel room, which he wasn't even sure he'd be doing. So he sat at the STRAT hotel's casino bar, sipping a root beer float, and waiting for a burger, his laptop open before him. The STRAT was just a baby step up from Circus, Circus, which he knew he couldn't take—too many squealing kids—and it fit the county's budget.

Doctors…nurses…pharmacists maybe, he thought, as he scrolled down through pages of testimony. There was a dermatologist over in Salt Lake City whose practice had turned its 401(k) over to Hamilton to invest—or, at least, to recommend the funds that employees could choose from. Hamilton had invested the employer's portion of the plan. The doc's name was Bingham, Tom Bingham. He and Brad met on the chair lift at Deer Valley, and he and his wife had dinner with Brad and Margie the following night, struck up a friendship, one thing led to another. But he had been called as a character witness for the defense, talked about what a great guy Hamilton was, and how well the retirement funds had done. One of the lucky ones, hardly a suspect.

Tony finished his burger and paid his check. Then he headed for the airport, just twenty minutes away. He turned in the rental car and bought a ticket on the first available flight to Phoenix. *Back to my empty apartment.* As he lined up to board the plane, he found himself wondering if he should adopt a dog. A dog would be happy when he returned home.

Twenty-nine

"**KEY** Lime Pound Cake, seriously?" Margaret Chavez took the plate June offered her and beckoned her into the kitchen. She placed the cake—its powdered-sugar glaze sprinkled with lime zest—on the countertop, and gave her beautiful guest an air kiss on each cheek. Then she hugged her sister-in-law, and turned to pour three glasses of white wine. She handed one to each of the other women and raised her own in a toast.

"TGIF," June said, adding, "thank you so much for including me."

"TGIF," Maria and Margaret responded.

Scottie and Ginny came tumbling into the kitchen at that moment, heading toward Maria. She set her glass down and took a twin under each arm, squeezing them tightly. They smiled shyly at June, who smiled back, and then eyed the cake.

"Yum," they said in unison. "What's TGIF?"

"Thank goodness it's Friday," said Maria. "Now, let me go find *mi madre* and give her a kiss, then you girls must tell your Tia Maria everything new in your lives."

The three exited the kitchen, leaving June and Margaret to sip their wine and make small talk.

"Is there anything new at the clinic?"

"Not really," June said. "I know it's a premier place to work and all, but in some ways, for me at least, it's just a job. To be honest with you, I'm feeling a little homesick. I think that would change, though, if I were to meet a man." She smiled at Margaret and gave a quick wink.

Before Margaret could respond, the back door opened, and Frank entered.

"Surprise!" said June.

"Surprise, indeed," said Frank. "It's nice to see you, June. How have you been?" He removed his hat and hung it on its hook, then touched June lightly on the arm.

"Since my last fiasco, you mean? Fine, thank you, and thank you again so much for your help, Frank. I am trying very hard not to do one more stupid thing that wastes your time."

"I'm always happy to help if I can," Frank said, giving Margaret a kiss before he pulled the refrigerator door open for a beer. "Where is everyone?"

"With your mother," Margaret said. "Dinner will be ready shortly."

"I'll let them know."

"Dinnertime!" Frank announced, as he headed down the hall.

Thirty

"THAT was delicious, Margaret. May I clear the dishes and cut some cake?" June said.

"We'll get the dishes—you cut the cake. We're all dying to try it! I'll put on a pot of decaf."

While the coffee brewed, Maria and the twins removed dirty dinner plates from the table, and June delivered dessert plates with generous slices of the pound cake she finally admitted she had made from scratch, using an old *Southern Living* recipe.

"Tell us about your visit with your daughter, June," said Margaret, as she pushed one remaining cake crumb from her plate onto her finger and brought it to her mouth, licking it and smiling with pleasure.

"It was great, once we got back on track. You know, Greg and I used to tease each other when our daughter was little. I'd take her in her stroller to the mall, and as we walked out the door he'd say, 'Be careful not to lose the baby!'

"Or, he'd take her with him to watch a practice, once he was coaching, to give me a break, and I'd warn him not to lose the baby. It was just a little joke between us. But that night…I was terrified I might be calling to tell him that, somehow, I'd gone and done it."

Margaret nodded sympathetically, sneaking a protective glance at her own daughters.

"Anyway, Savannah and I had spa treatments at the hotel, and we spent the better part of an afternoon shopping at Fashion Square. We went into Phoenix one evening and saw a show. We packed a lot of fun into three days, and had some good mother-daughter talks, too, mostly about her studies, but also about how her dad is doing."

"Savannah is studying neurology," Maria explained to her brother and his family. "That girl is sweet, pretty, *and* smart."

"Neurology," Frank said. "How did she choose that subject?"

"She's been interested in it for years, ever since I decided we had to get away from Greg, after his behavior became so erratic."

"I see," Frank said.

It was suddenly quiet around the table.

"Girls," Margaret said, "I think you told me you had some math homework. Why don't you go get started on it now, before it gets to be too late."

The twins left the table, thanking June for the cake and hugging their aunt on the way to their room. Aurelia had nodded off, her chin lowered to her chest, and Frank gently led her away as well.

"I'm sorry," June said, "I didn't mean to end this lovely dinner party on a negative note. As I've explained to Frank, my former husband wasn't a mean person. What happened to him wasn't his fault."

"Please don't apologize," Margaret said. "And the dinner party doesn't need to end!"

"We really should go," June said, with a nod to Maria. "But the cake stays."

Margaret protested, but gave in when she saw that June was determined.

She hugged each of the women goodbye and stood with her arm around Frank as Maria's car pulled away from the curb.

Thirty-one

"**WHAT** the f-?!" Frank gasped under his breath as he jumped out of bed and flung himself toward the bathroom. "Jesus, Mary and Joseph..." He yanked the shower curtain back and turned the water on full blast.

"What is it honey?" he heard Margaret murmur dreamily from the bedroom. It sounded like she was asleep, and he sincerely hoped she was, but he went to her and answered, just in case.

"Nothing, babe," he whispered. "I have an early start today. You just keep sleeping." It was four o'clock in the morning, and Frank had no idea what he was going to do with himself between now and sunrise, but he sure as hell wasn't going back to bed.

He had been making love to his wife, kissing her lips and gently biting her earlobes, making his way from her neck to her breasts. And then, it was June he was having sex with, his pleasant dream mutating into pure night terror.

"Please forgive me, Jesus," he whispered, as the water poured over him, "for taking your name in vain. And for the f-bomb, too. Dear God, it was a dream. I love my wife, you know I do. I would never be unfaithful to her. June is a friend. It was a dream. I love my wife…"

Thirty-two

NANCY Scott, her husband, Ben Witkowski, and John and Jennifer Crouch sat on stools at a high-top table in the bar at the Saddle Bronc Grill in Fountain Hills. It was Saturday night, and the place was hopping, every monitor tuned to a different college football game. Ben told his wife he was craving chicken-fried steak, and the group agreed to indulge him. The women ordered the chicken green chili stew, and John was having a burger, the John Wayne Cheese, a local favorite. They shared a pitcher of Spellbinder.

"So what's new in Denver?" John said. Ben had an architecture practice in Colorado and commuted back and forth between there and his home in Arizona.

"Same old, same old," Ben said. "What's new here? Business still good?"

"Never better." John knocked his right knuckles on the nearest wooden surface.

"So, John, I have a question for you," Nancy said. "Did you ever know a guy named Bradley Hamilton?"

"I know *of* him. Knew of him I should say. I heard he died recently. Why do you ask?"

"The authorities think he was murdered."

"Yeah, that's what I read.'"

"He was in financial services, right?" Jennifer said. "Did he do the same things you do?"

"He did," John said, "only, dishonestly. Fact is, I think he talked to the McDougals at one point, but they wanted nothing to do with him. By then, the companies he worked with were starting to get suspicious. Things get around. Anyway, he was caught and went to prison. When something like that happens, it's bad for the whole profession—makes people think they can't trust us, and trust is what we sell. That, and competency."

"Well, it's weird," Nancy said, "but the deputy sheriff over in Carefree called me recently. Frank Chavez had suggested he talk to me, because of my novel and all."

"Oh, yeah," John said, "Rancho Manana—that's where they found Hamilton, right?"

"Right. I've been going back through the book with a fine-tooth comb, trying to pick up on anything that might be helpful."

Thirty-three

TONY Block walked out of Terminal Four at Sky Harbor and pulled up a car service app on his phone. He'd thought about asking Trevor for a ride—he would have come for him—but there was no reason to interrupt his evening. He just hoped he had something to eat in the refrigerator at home. He honestly couldn't remember; it seemed like he had been away for weeks, though it had been less than one. During that time he had talked to upwards of twenty of Brad Hamilton's former clients, either in person or on the phone. All nice people, but they were starting to run together in his mind.

When Tony turned the key in the lock and opened his front door, he saw that he had accidentally left the kitchen light on, and there were moths flickering around it. Things smelled a little musty, but other than that, it was as he had left it. *Be it ever so humble...*

And praise the Lord, he had two different TV dinners to choose from. He turned the oven to four hundred and removed the cellophane wrapping from the fried chicken and mashed potato option. It wouldn't be as good as The Horny Toad's—no way near—but he was glad to be home, sitting at his own kitchen table, and looking forward to spending the night in his own bed.

He decided to go down to the box and collect his mail while the oven preheated. Back at the table, he shuffled through the flyers and envelopes, mostly solicitations, nothing first class, nothing from Lizzy. The fact was, he hadn't heard from Lizzy in months. But he always hoped she would write, or call, or email, or something. Most of the mail he had retrieved went into the recycle bin next to the trash can, unopened.

He scarfed down his dinner and crashed, without even undressing.

Thirty-four

"So. What do you have?" said Trevor, sitting across from Tony at the First Watch in Carefree, waiting for their breakfast orders to arrive.

"I hate to admit it, but not much. Hamilton was smart, likeable, inspired trust in people, invested their money, elevated his lifestyle, got in over his head, started stealing his clients' money to pay his own bills, went to jail, was a model prisoner, got out, and got himself killed—probably by someone he knew. That's it in a nutshell. You?"

"Jack went through his bank statements. Normal debits—rent, utilities. Didn't eat out. Minimal pump charges, groceries, that kind of thing. The car parked at his apartment in Reno—we don't know yet where he got it. Or, I should say, we don't know where he got the money to pay for it. We found the charge for his plane ticket, on Southwest, round-trip, Reno to Phoenix. Obviously, he only used half of it. No clue as to why he was here."

"Job interview, maybe?" Tony said. "Rendezvous with a former partner, a fellow prisoner, a girlfriend? Margie, his ex-wife, told me their kids are settled in the Midwest, both married, with kids of their own. They've forgiven their dad, but they don't really have anything to do with him. Sad."

"One of them could have loaned him some money, though. For the car, I mean," Trevor said.

"Yeah, maybe. I'll call Margie and ask if she knows. By the way, I'm getting a dog." Tony had previously only considered this idea, but now he found himself committing to it.

"Really. What kind?"

"Not sure, a mutt probably. One no one else wants."

"Why don't you get a girlfriend instead?"

"I don't know. A dog seems easier."

"Yeah, I hear ya."

Thirty-five

"**SAVANNAH?** Am I catching you at a good time?"

"Sure, Momma, what's up?"

"Well, I don't want to get overly excited about this, but I had a date with a wonderful guy last week. Since then, I've seen him almost every night, and it's, I don't know, it just seems like we really have a lot in common. Actually, I'm not sure about that, but the chemistry is definitely there. And he treats me like a princess."

"That's great! How did you meet him?"

"Online, which I know can be iffy, judging from my past experiences. In fact, I swore I'd never go to a dating website again. But then I decided to take a chance, and I'm glad I did. Anyway, it's over a month away, but I was wondering…well, what if I invited Ray—that's his name—to go with us to Puerta Vallarta? I mean, I would only invite him if you said it was okay. And maybe there's someone you'd like to invite."

"Well, sure, if that's what you'd like to do. I can't think of anyone I'd ask, but that doesn't mean you shouldn't."

"Thanks, honey. I'm not sure yet, but I thought I'd check with you. How's your dad, any news?"

"Daddy's gotten into a therapy trial, and I think it's promising. We'll see. I'll tell him you asked about him."

"Yes, do. Well, I'll let you get back to your studies now. I love you."

"I love you too, Momma."

Thirty-six

"So tell me, June," Ray said, smiling at her from across the table at Grassroots Kitchen in Scottsdale, where they had just enjoyed cocktails and dinner, "do you have plans for the weekend?"

June studied Ray's face. She wondered briefly if he had veneers—his teeth were perfectly straight, and amazingly white. His deep blue eyes crinkled at the corners, and he had dimples in both cheeks. He was so good-looking, her heart skipped a beat.

"None that can't be changed, if the offer is good enough." She hoped she sounded coy. The truth was her plans for Saturday had been to do laundry, shop for groceries, and clean the bathroom, nothing that couldn't be postponed indefinitely. *When does the weekend start anyway, tomorrow night, or Saturday morning?*

"I was thinking about a day hike up to the Camelback early Saturday, and then a swim at my place. We could put some steaks on the grill there later."

"That sounds like fun. And I heard the forecast is good—not too hot, and no rain. I'd love to join you."

"Great. I'll plan to pick you up at seven in the morning, with a thermos of coffee for the drive. It'll take us forty-five minutes to get to the trailhead. Be sure to put on sunscreen and wear a hat. I don't want to be responsible for any damage to that flawless skin."

She glowed at the compliment. Like most Southern women, she had spent a lifetime protecting her skin from overexposure to the sun, and it was nice to have the effort appreciated.

"I should probably be getting home now," she said. "I work the early shift on Fridays. Thank you for a lovely evening. I'll be looking forward to Saturday."

Thirty-seven

"So, if you don't mind my asking, what caused the breakup between you and your former husband?"

June and Ray were on the trail, ascending at a good pace, neither of them too winded from the exertion to converse while climbing.

"Well, as I said, we had been high-school sweethearts, and when he was recruited to play football at the university, in Chapel Hill, I followed him there. Those were still the days when women went to college to get an MRS, at least, in the part of the country where I grew up. Greg played center, and he sustained multiple head injuries—both in high school, and in college. No one paid that much attention then. If a boy could get up and get back onto the field, great. The crowd just cheered them on.

"Greg had a sweet personality. When I told him I was pregnant halfway through our junior year, he was elated. He met with my father immediately and asked for my hand in marriage, and my mother began to plan our wedding. Of course, neither of my parents were thrilled, but that had nothing to do with Greg. It was just the stigma, you know, that existed in their social group.

"But when Savannah was born, oh, my goodness, none of the grandparents could keep their hands off her. Greg continued playing—it was paying his way, after all. After graduation, he got a good job, with a little club coaching on the side, and things were fine. But as our daughter got older, her father became more and more impatient with her. And he would yell at me too, for no cause. His own father was a dear man, so it wasn't that he had grown up around abuse. But over time, he became just that— abusive. It's hard for me to say it, even today. I sought help. The professionals I talked to theorized it was traumatic brain injuries, coming back to haunt him, and suggested forbearance. I tried.

"But when I stopped feeling safe in my own home, I left, and of course, took Savannah with me. I still care for the man, and Savannah loves her father very much. But I can't be married to him."

"I'm sorry," Ray said, putting his arm around June's shoulder and gently pulling her toward him.

"Thank you," she said. "I could use a water break as soon as we get to that patch of shade."

Later, at Ray's house, June undressed in the room he had shown her to and slipped into her tankini. She pulled her hair into a high ponytail, and studied her image in the full-length mirror, tucking her buttocks and sucking in her gut. She knew she was attractive—people told her so—but still, she was a forty-two-year-old woman, who had given birth, in a bathing suit…

Might as well face the music. She stepped from the bedroom through the French doors onto the landscaped terrace where the pool shone like a jewel. She had grown up between the country club and her family's beach house in the Outer Banks, and she was comfortable around water. She walked gracefully to the deep end and dove in, swimming the length of the pool. When she stood up, she saw that Ray watched her admiringly, holding a tray with two martinis in his hand.

"That drink looks better than any swim team medal I ever won," she said.

She exited at the shallow end and took a glass from the tray, which Ray set down on a table. He raised the other glass to hers.

"Cheers," they said in unison. "To us," he continued, and drew her body toward him, kissing her deeply, his tongue salty and tasting of olives, his bare, sculpted chest firm and warm. She shivered with pleasure. He put his drink back on the tray and wrapped her in an oversized towel, leading her to a lounge chair and taking her drink from her. He kissed her again, and she embraced him, wrapping her arms around his neck and pulling him in. After a minute that felt to her like an eternity, he handed her drink back to her and dove into the pool, visibly aroused.

Later, lying together in Ray's bed, sipping a second martini and looking out onto the terrace, June chided him. "About that steak you were going to grill for me…"

"Ah, yes, that wasn't a loss leader, I promise. It's just that you are such a distraction. I'm going to do it right now. Put on this robe, please, and keep me company while I cook. And try not to be such a fox until after we've eaten. Dinner, I mean."

She smiled demurely, and, wearing only the robe Ray had handed her, followed him to the kitchen, where she sat on a bar stool and watched him take two seasoned steaks from the refrigerator and place them next to the grill. He selected a bottle of red from a wine cooler and opened and decanted it. Then, he emptied a bag of salad greens into a wooden bowl, dressing the mixture lightly with a virgin olive oil and a grinding of salt and pepper.

June found herself smiling again. *Proficient in bed* and *in the kitchen*. It just kept getting better.

Their appetites whetted, they ate heartily. Looking into June's eyes across the candlelit table on the patio, where earlier he had turned the heat lamps on low, Ray told her, "I really should be a gentleman and offer to take you home now."

"Yes, you should. Or, I could call a car."

"Or," he said, his voice husky, "you could stay the night."

Thirty-eight

JUNE woke early, disoriented for a moment before remembering the night before, and the man sleeping next to her. A wave of pleasure coursed through her body, its destination her most erogenous zone, although she had spent the past twelve hours discovering ones she hadn't known she had. She thought of seducing Ray out of his slumber but decided to brush her teeth and take a quick shower first, which had the effect of calming her desire slightly. He was still sound asleep, so she decided to take in her surroundings in the morning light.

His home was a sprawling ranch with a long, open floor plan—a stacked brick fireplace at one end of the main room, and the spacious kitchen at the other. An island, with bar stools that faced the kitchen, served as a divider between the two.

The house was in an old, established neighborhood, where the homes were sited on five-acre lots, tall palms and citrus fruit trees defining their boundaries. June learned these details from thumbing through an issue of *Scottsdale City Lifestyle*, one of several magazines arranged on a hammered copper coffee table in front of an upholstered sofa with contrasting cushions. A worn leather chair, with an alpaca throw casually draped over its arm, sat on the opposite side of the table. A floor lamp and a basket holding more magazines was located to one side. The stone floor was softened by hand-knotted rugs that defined the areas.

On one of their evenings out, June had asked Ray about his work. According to his brief response, he graduated from business school and went to work for a medical billing service, purchasing the company from its founder after a few years and expanding it into multiple states. He was retired now, for the most part, although he still maintained various business interests. June didn't ask his age, but she estimated he was about twenty years her senior. He told her he had never married and had no children.

No exes, no baggage. Financially successful, by all appearances. Handsome, fit, and a generous lover...

She decided to make a pot of coffee. She was sipping a cup outside by the pool when Ray joined her, showered and shaved, shirtless, and holding his own steaming mug. She smiled at him, suddenly shy. He sat next to her, leaning over to kiss her gently on the lips.

"Good morning," he said.

"Good morning."

"The coffee's just right."

"Thank you, I tried not to make it too strong."

"It's perfect. Tell me, June Lambreth, what would you like to have for breakfast?"

Thirty-nine

"HEY, there, how was your weekend?" Maria set her lunch tray down, removing small plates of chicken salad and cottage cheese to the table before pulling out a chair next to June, who was just finishing the lunch it appeared she had packed at home.

"It was heavenly."

"Yes…say more. Something tells me you and that man you met are getting along nicely."

"Nicely, yes, or naughtily," June said, laughing, "or maybe swimmingly. Let's just say that he and I spent the better part of the weekend together, and I'm smitten. I think it's mutual."

"Well, I'm happy for you, and maybe just a little bit jealous. I wouldn't mind meeting a man myself. I just can't do the online thing, even though I've heard lots of success stories. Good for you, girlfriend!"

"Who knows, Maria? Maybe Ray has a best friend who's looking for a beautiful girl like you. We could have a double wedding!"

"LOL, let's not get carried away. Wait a minute. You're serious, aren't you?"

"I'm seriously hopeful. Greg and I have been divorced for over seven years now, and I would like nothing more than to meet a man to share the rest of my life with. Of course, it would have to be someone Savannah likes. I asked how she would feel about Ray joining us at Christmas. She sounded a little hesitant."

"That's normal, I assume. From what I've read, when parents divorce, the kids always hold out hope they might get back together. Remarriage eliminates that possibility. But she's such a lovely girl, I know that, whenever it happens, she'll be happy for you."

"I'm sure you're right. Well, I'd better get back to work."

Forty

"So, working theory—and only because we don't have a better one—is that our man, Hamilton, was in the area for a meeting, maybe a job interview. According to his bank records, he was collecting Social Security, the benefit he could apply for at sixty-two, and he had been out of the work force for twenty years, so not that much money. And he was knocked off by someone he knew, maybe someone in the medical profession." Trevor Smith and Tony Block were back at the First Watch, this time with Jack Powell.

"Reasonable," Jack responded to Trevor's summary of their limited facts. "According to the resort, his reservation had come through one of those third-party booking agencies, a deal at the last minute. It's not as though he had a golf vacation in mind. I think that was coincidental. His plane ticket was purchased earlier."

"So, who was he meeting, and is that the person who gave him the shot?" Trevor asked the two, his mounting frustration apparent. He had total confidence in these deputies, but a breakthrough in the case was overdue.

"I called Margie," Tony said. "She's Hamilton's ex-wife," he added, for Jack's benefit. "She didn't know anything about a car. Said maybe one of the kids lent him the money for one, but she didn't think so. But she said if they did, they might not want to tell her. She's asking 'em and getting back to me. I'm not sure if I was reading her right, but my sense is she feels guilty about letting their lifestyle get out of hand, and about not smelling the coffee around how her husband was dealing with it. She might even feel guilty about his death."

Forty-one

"**Hi,** Nancy."

"Jennifer! I haven't seen you in ages! I'm sorry, I've neglected our friendship. I'm hard at work on this book, but I'm stuck. Wanna walk?"

"Sure. And no worries. I'll head out in five."

"Me too!" Nancy pulled on her cross-trainers and closed the door behind her—no need to lock it for the short time she'd be gone. She and her best friend had established a regular walking route through the neighborhood that took her an hour, door to door. She hugged Jennifer when they met, and the two fell into lockstep.

"So, other than putting words on paper, what's happening in your life?" Jennifer asked.

"Well, Ben's here again this weekend, so let's get together then for sure. And my mother is paying us a visit—coming all the way from Ohio—in two weeks. She'll want to see you, of course."

"I'd love to see your mother. How long is she staying, and how are you planning to entertain her?"

"One week. The usual—the MIM, The Heard…"

"Fun. Please consider bringing her over to Harrington House. You won't believe how much we have going on, with some good outside speakers on the docket, too." Jennifer was referring to the non-profit listening center she had conceived of and brought into being using funds she had inherited from her dear friends, Dick and Shirley Harrington. The Mayo Clinic Foundation and McDougal Partners, her husband's employer, had also been major contributors.

"Absolutely! I'll go to the website and see which of your guest speakers coordinates with Mom's visit. Now about this weekend, what should we do for fun? Maybe the putting course—with cocktails, naturally—and then dinner on the clubhouse patio?"

"Sounds perfect. I'll make a reservation; you stay focused on your writing. I keep meaning to ask, how are sales from the first book going?"

"Sales are good, reviews are good. And I'm getting invitations to book club meetings, so all good. But…I can't stop thinking about that murder over at Rancho Manana…"

Forty-two

"CHEERS!" Nancy said, as four plastic glasses clunked together on the Tonto Verde putting course at the first hole. The foursome played the course in seventy-five minutes, with no shortage of laughter and a few small bets, then returned the putters to their golf carts and headed through the grill to the hostess station to check in and be led to their table.

More drinks were ordered, and the two couples relaxed into their comfortable chairs under the warmth of the overhead heaters, enjoying the last glow of the late fall sunset.

"Well, I'm not sorry for this week to be over," John Crouch announced to the group.

Ben raised one eyebrow in question.

"It wasn't very productive is all," John explained. "We had our annual compliance meeting, and also the required training on current scams, money laundering schemes, et cetera. The people who perpetrate these crimes get bolder and more creative all the time. Honestly, if my parents were still around, I'd be terrified for them to pick up the phone—or use their computers, for that matter."

"You hear a lot of stories, that's for sure," Jennifer said. "Some of the Lady Putters have shared them…"

"Explain the money-laundering part," Ben said. "That's something I've never quite understood."

"It has to do with money that's been acquired through illegal activity—drug dealing, sex trafficking, tax evasion, corporate embezzlement—huge amounts of money, in some cases, that can't be easily spent without raising red flags. First, it has to be integrated into the economy in a legit way. So, traffickers, or mules—which are people knowingly, or sometimes unknowingly, hired to do it—open multiple bank accounts and deposit the maximum amount of cash allowed without the bank being required to notify the feds. Or, they use a wire transfer to buy a big life insurance policy, for example, or apply for an annuity contract. Those are things I sell. That phase is called 'placement.' Then they shuffle things around, trying to create distance between them and the funds. That's called 'layering.' It gets confusing."

"The max they can deposit is ten thousand, right?" Nancy said.

"Cash, right," John said. "Finally, the crooks retrieve the money for their own uses—homes, cars, expensive watches, whatever. But now it's clean. That's why they call it 'laundering.'"

"It never ceases to amaze me, the ways some people come up with to be dishonest. Why not apply that brain power to legitimate work?" Nancy scratched her head, as if to physically illustrate her point.

"I hear you," John said. "Bottom line is that people who do what I do are required to get specialized training in how to recognize the signs of this kind of activity. It's fascinating, actually. But, like I said, it didn't make for a very productive week."

Forty-three

"ANYTHING new at the clinic?" Frank asked Maria, as the whole family clustered in the Chavez living room. The twins lay prone on the floor, heads resting on crossed arms, almost touching. As usual, they shared a history book. Frank didn't know how his daughters managed to read in sync, but they did. Must be a twin thing.

His mother had nodded off in her chair, her magazine slipping from her lap. Frank's sister, and his wife, each held a glass of white wine, and Frank drank beer from a bottle. A pot of beef stew simmered on the stove in the kitchen, the aroma of its rich tomato-based broth wafting through the small house. Jackson Browne sang *Running on Empty* through the smart speaker, its volume turned low.

"Not with work, per se. But I do have news about June. She has a boyfriend."

"Really?" Frank said. "How did she meet him?" Ever since his terrifying dream, he had managed not to think about June Lambreth. He knew it was meaningless, but still…

"Online, how else?" Maria said. "I'm cautiously optimistic. According to June, he's wonderful—tall, dark, and handsome. Ray something or other. In her words, she's 'smitten'. I just hope she'll take her time about getting into anything too serious."

"Well, I for one couldn't be happier for her," Margaret said. "We'll have to have them both over, so we can meet this man and give them both our blessing."

Frank looked at his watch. "Is that stew ready to eat? I'm starving. Sorry, Sis," he said sheepishly, "I don't mean to be rude. I had a light lunch."

"No worries. I need to go. I'm joining a discussion group, over at Harrington House. For millennials."

"Really," said Margaret. "I hadn't heard."

"I just signed up for it. I figure if June's not going to be available to hang out with anymore, I need to meet some new friends. Wish me luck!" Maria bent to kiss her mother, then the girls. "Thanks for the wine," she said, giving a little wave as she let herself out.

Forty-four

"**HEY** June-bug," Ray said, his voice throaty. "Do you have a minute?"

"I have all the time in the world for you," she whispered into the phone, although it wasn't true. She was expected at a meeting down the hall in just a few minutes. She sighed. Work was starting to get in the way of her new romance. She imagined Ray sitting in his sunlit great room, leaning back in his chair, his laptop open, a glass of diet cola sweating on a coaster next to it. Now that would be the way to work.

"Good to know," he said. "I was wondering, what would you like to do for dinner tonight? We could cook here, or order out. Or, I could take you over to Paradise Valley, the Jade Bar, maybe?"

"Ooh, that sounds nice." What she really wanted to do was climb into Ray's bed and never leave, but she answered, "Whatever you choose is fine with me. I'm afraid I lied—I need to go. Would you text me the plan? I'll stop by my place to change, and be there as soon as I can, probably around six-thirty, with traffic. I'll be ready for a cold adult beverage."

"You've got it."

June sprinted down the hall, sliding into the one empty seat at the conference table as the doc in charge closed the door and addressed the small group. His tone was grave. A well-known actor had flown over from Los Angeles for an executive physical—a day-long process that carried a price tag of anywhere from five to ten thousand dollars—and her examiners observed discoloration of her left breast. In the short time she had been in the hospital, small dimples began to appear, and although further testing was inconclusive, the consensus was that she had recently developed inflammatory breast cancer, which had most likely already spread to her lymph nodes.

"As you all know, this form is one of the most aggressive ones out there. And sadly, it favors African American women. Our star has coronary artery disease to boot. The Mayo has put together a top-drawer care team to help her fight back as hard as those cancer cells are attacking. You are each an important member of that team."

Forty-five

"AND you can't even give me a hint?" Ray said.

June shook her head. "I'm sorry, Ray, I can't. Patient confidentiality. I probably shouldn't have said as much as I did, but this is going to have me a little distracted, and I don't want you to think it's anything between us." She leaned across the table and kissed him lightly. "Forgive me?"

"There's nothing to forgive. I understand." He shrugged his shoulders, then gave her the smile that made electricity course through her body. "Anything on the menu look good to you?"

They sat at the Jade Bar at Sanctuary Camelback Mountain, drinking martinis and sharing a Baja Shrimp Cocktail. This particular venue at the resort and spa was walk-in only. It was best to arrive by four if you wanted to be assured of finding two seats together—either early, or after eight. Because of June's meeting, and her need to unpack it when she arrived at Ray's, they were on the late side of the window. They found a quiet corner table, and June studied the menu.

"I'm not that hungry," she finally answered. "Maybe the beet salad…"

"Sounds good. I'll give you a slice of my steak, and maybe even a couples of fries, in exchange for a bite of something green."

"It's a deal."

She relaxed, taking a sip of her drink, reaching across the table to take his hand. She and Ray had been together for three weeks now, and it seemed to her they had known each other forever. He continued to treat her like royalty, and she was learning to accept being placed on a pedestal. After all, she had grown up in the South, where women—white women, at least—were naturally revered. But they weren't always treated as equal to their male counterparts, able to make their own decisions about things that affected them personally. And now, with the Supreme Court ruling that reversed Roe v. Wade, many southern states threatened to take women back to the days before June was even born.

Several times, she had thought Ray was about to ask her to move in with him, and she hadn't been sure what she would say. As much time as she spent at his house, it might make sense. But their relationship was still new, and she liked having her own space. Of course, money was always tight for her, so there were financial considerations. Her mother used to say, "Why buy the cow, when you can have the milk for free?" June had hated that saying, but it was a good reminder that if Ray wanted her badly enough, he should—in the words that had made almost ten million dollars for Beyoncé—put a ring on it.

June finished her dinner and excused herself to visit the powder room. She freshened her lipstick and checked her hair before returning. As she made her way back through the bar toward their table, smiling at Ray as she approached, she noticed a party of four intent on their discussion—heads leaning in to catch each other's words—just a few tables over. They had fresh drinks in front of them, their menus unopened. One of the women had flaming red hair and spoke more loudly, and with more animation, than the others.

Nancy Scott, the author. June had seen her interviewed by a local book seller on his YouTube channel. Shyly, she approached their table and introduced herself as an admirer.

"I read your book recently on the recommendation of my friend, Maria Chavez," she said.

"Frank's sister! We're friends!" Nancy said. "I'm so flattered you recognized me! Can you join us? This is my husband, Ben, and our friends, Jennifer and John. We just attended a book talk at The Poisoned Pen, in Old Town."

The two men leapt to their feet, and Jennifer smiled and extended her hand.

June pointed toward her own table. "My boyfriend's waiting for me. We're leaving soon. But thank you so much for the invitation."

All four smiled in Ray's direction.

"Thank you for stopping to introduce yourself!" Nancy said.

"What a beauty," June overheard Jennifer say as she walked away. "I wonder where in the South *she's* from." The compliment both buoyed and embarrassed her.

Ray frowned when she returned to their table. "Who are they?" he asked.

June smiled. *Was he the possessive type?* "Nancy Scott, an author friend of the Chavez family, and her friends. I recently read a book she wrote."

"I see. I've handled the check, shall we go?" He stood to pull June's chair and led her from the room. He seemed to steer her away from the two couples she had just met.

He does *want me all to himself.* June smiled again, treasuring the thought…

Forty-six

"**THIS** six-week course was described in the online brochure as 'Listening to Your Inner Voice', with a focus on how that comes into play in our relationships, particularly relationships with intimate partners."

Maria listened attentively as the woman who had introduced herself simply as Camille spoke to the group of twelve adults seated around the casual living room at Harrington House. Comfortable sofas in various neutral shades, and matching chairs, were arranged to facilitate conversation. The lighting was soft and ambient.

"There are just a few basic rules of engagement. One, listen respectfully to each other. Two, exercise confidentiality. And three, be kind." Camille went on to explain that she was a psychologist with a practice in marriage and family counseling; then, she invited the others to introduce themselves.

Maria waited for someone to speak. When no one did, she took the initiative.

"My name is Maria. My pronouns are she/her. I'm a cardiology nurse, single, no kids, no pets, two adorable nieces. I'm not exactly sure why I signed up to participate," she said, smiling self-consciously. "I'm not in a relationship, and the truth is, I've never been in one, not a serious one, that is. I guess maybe that's the reason I'm here, to find out if something is holding me back."

She saw the others nodding their support. She had broken the ice, and one by one they took their turns.

"My name is Tony, and I'm an orphan." Maria smiled encouragingly as the speaker, who she found good-looking, gave a self-deprecating laugh. "My mother died of cancer when I was five. My dad remarried when I was in high school, then he and my stepmom died in a car accident when I was in college. She had a daughter, Lizzy, whom I was close to. Maybe too close. Anyway, I haven't seen my stepsister in five years, and it's clear she doesn't want to reconnect. I'm trying to get over her rejection, but I'm stuck."

Forty-seven

"So, baby, can I talk you into spending the night with me?" Ray pulled into the double driveway next to June's car and activated the garage door opener, parking the Porsche 911 next to an older model Mercedes sedan.

"You know I'd like to," June said, smiling. "But I need to get to the clinic even earlier than usual tomorrow. May I have a raincheck?" She leaned over to kiss him on the cheek, but he turned his head away.

Surprised and hurt, she thought about changing her mind. She could set an alarm and leave before the traffic got heavy, stop by her condo to change and pack her lunch, and still get to work in time to greet her new charge before the doctors' rounds. Should she give in to Ray's mood, or stick with her original plan?

"How about we go inside and talk about it?" she suggested. Her compromise was rewarded with a brilliant smile. Ray killed the engine and stepped around the sports car to open June's door, helping her out, and drawing her into his arms for a kiss.

Inside, she watched him take the martini shaker from the bar cart and mix and pour two drinks. He handed one to her before leading her to the sofa and dimming the lights. June took a sip, and knew immediately that if she finished the drink, which seemed even stronger than the ones she had imbibed earlier, it would be unsafe for her to drive home that night. She chided herself for her lack of willpower, for seeking Ray's approval at the expense of her own resolve. But she pushed these thoughts aside as he began kissing her and slowly caressing her body with his free hand, feeling it come alive to his touch, giving in to the pleasure. She would not be going anywhere, at least not anytime soon.

Forty-eight

"GOOD morning," said June softly, the rubber soles of her white leather shoes barely making footfalls as she approached the patient in Room Eleven, whose hospital bed was raised to a half-elevated position. The room was dark, although it was eight o'clock in the morning, but when she got closer, June could see that Ms. Doe's eyelids were open. Ms. Doe, Jane Doe, was how the staff had agreed to refer to their glamourous patient. *Seriously? Couldn't we have come up with something a little more original?*

"May I open your drapes and let in a little Arizona sunshine? It's a beautiful day." How banal, she thought, talking about the weather to someone recently diagnosed with one of the most serious forms of cancer in the American Cancer Society's guidebook.

"That would be lovely, thank you. Then please come a little closer, so I can see your face."

June opened the drapes, then neared the bedside, smiling. "May I order some breakfast for you, a cup of coffee? My name is June, June Lambreth."

"It's nice to meet you, June. I've had a cup already, and one is my limit. I understand I am to be on a special diet while I'm here. I'm ready for breakfast anytime. And thank you for letting in the light. It's amazing, the simple things we take for granted. That's something I hope to change about myself in this present moment—taking natural beauty, and beautiful people, for granted."

June smiled her appreciation, then picked up the phone to call the food service manager. One of the things the clinic prided itself on was the excellent cuisine it provided to patients and visitors alike, regardless of dietary considerations. She knew Jane Doe would be served small meals throughout the day—high in protein, vitamins and minerals—during the time she had her initial chemotherapy, which would be followed by her mastectomy. This was one of the reasons for the secrecy. A Hollywood star, famous for her beauty and her body, was about to lose her breasts.

"Can I do anything to make you more comfortable while you wait for your food to arrive?" June asked.

"Maybe tell me a little about yourself. Where are you from?"

"Charlotte, originally," June answered.

"I knew it! You have the same accent I had, before all those voice lessons my agent insisted on. And while we're at it, please call me Jae. My real name is Jacqueline, but my mother and my brother always called me Jae. I understand I'm Jane Doe around here, and you-know-who to the rest of the world, but if I understand the program, you and I are going to be seeing a lot of each other. So, let's be soul sisters from Charlotte—June and Jae."

"Deal." June laughed, giving Jae a little hug. She took her patient's vitals and entered them into the hospital room's computer, keeping up a stream of small talk as she worked. It turned out that she and Jae had much more in common than a hometown.

There was a short rap on the door before it was pushed open and the doorstop pulled into place. An orderly wheeled a cart toward Jae's bed, atop it a tray bearing a luncheon-size china plate with a small spinach omelet, a thin slice of whole wheat toast, and a mixed berry compote attractively arranged on it. A crystal vase with a single pink rose anchored the top left-hand corner, a small glass of orange juice filled the opposite one. A white linen napkin and sparkling silverware completed the presentation.

Jae smiled at the server. "Am I in the hospital, or dining at a five-star restaurant?"

Star-struck, the young man returned the smile, backing out of the room as he spoke. "Please let us know if we can bring you anything else, Ms. Doe."

Forty-nine

JUNE sat with Maria in the cafeteria at half past noon, the early lunch crowd beginning to thin out, the later one starting to trickle in. She'd emptied her paper lunch sack and folded it neatly for reuse tomorrow.

"How's it going?" asked her friend.

"Fine," June said, "although I could use a nap about now." She didn't elaborate, but she thought Maria could probably tell she was fatigued, and possibly still a little hung over.

"Your patient doing okay today?"

"She's lovely," June said. "If grace and charm matter at all, she's going to beat this thing."

"Well let's pray she does; talent like hers doesn't come along every day."

"No, it doesn't. I think I've seen every movie she's ever made. My daughter likes her, too."

"How is Savannah? Are you still going to Mexico together at Christmas?"

"The last time I spoke with her she was fine, and the trip is definitely on. I think I told you I invited Ray to join us."

"That's awesome, I'm glad things are going well. My sister-in-law is making noise about wanting to meet your man friend, and I'm eager to meet him too. She suggested the two of you come up with some dates that would work for dinner."

"How kind of her, I'd love for Ray to meet you and your family. We'll look at our calendars tonight. I'd better go check on Jae—Jane, I mean. Thanks, Maria."

Fifty

June lay curled up on Ray's sofa, a tapestry pillow under her head, the alpaca throw wrapped around her body. The desert evenings were quite chilly of late. A log was blazing in the fireplace, and Ray was mixing drinks at the kitchen end of the great room. She was trying not to fall asleep before dinner, but she wasn't sure she would make it.

"Here you go, baby," Ray said, placing a chilled martini glass on the coffee table. "Cheers."

"Cheers," June smiled up at him. She knew she was drinking more lately than she should, more than she ever had in her life, and she had vowed that morning to make this an alcohol-free day, but her willpower had vanished the minute she walked through Ray's front door.

"Ray," she said, "I have some good friends—Maria Chavez, from work, her brother Frank, and his wife, Margaret. They want us to find some dates when we can join them all for dinner.

They'd like to meet you. And I want you to meet them. They're the closest thing I have here to family."

Ray leaned back against the opposite end of the sofa. He took a sip of his drink, and pulled one of his olives from its toothpick, studying it before popping it into his mouth, chewing and swallowing it as though deep in thought.

"I'll think about it, Junie."

"What? I mean, what is there to think about?"

"You know, baby, I'm perfectly content just having it be you and me. I don't feel the need to widen my circle of friends."

"But Ray, these are *my* friends. I would think you'd be eager to meet them."

"We'll see."

"But what should I tell them?"

He leaned forward and patted her knee. "You're a clever girl, I'm sure you'll come up with something. Let's finish our drinks, and then I'll open a special bottle of wine. We're having a creamy chicken and pasta dish. I think you'll like it."

Fifty-one

THE following morning, June opened the door to Jae's room and walked directly to the window, pulling the shades open to reveal the brilliant morning sunlight. She walked to the bed and took the woman's hand in hers.

"Good morning, Jae," she said.

"Good morning, June," Jae's voice sounded weaker than it had twenty-four hours before. "How was your evening?"

"Okay," June said. "And yours? Were you able to sleep?"

"I was, with a little help from my friends," Jae said, with a sheepish smile. June had overheard Jae's lead doctor tell the head night nurse that a small dose of Ambien was fine. Jae needed strength for the days that lay ahead. Rest was just as important as good nutrition.

"That's good," June said. "Tell me, is anyone coming to be with you during your treatment? The clinic has a lovely residence inn where visiting relatives can stay."

"I'm afraid not. I've been unlucky in love, or maybe just unsuccessful, on three different occasions. I have no children, which I guess is for the best. My brother needs to stay with our mother. She's aging in place, and doing quite well, all things considered. But she isn't well enough to travel, or to stay alone. What about you, sister? If you were in my place, who would be here, holding your hand?"

June hesitated. "I have a daughter, Savannah. She's a junior in college. She'd be here."

"A beauty like you, and no man in your life?"

"There is a man. His name is Ray. But, I'm not exactly sure. Where I stand with him, I mean."

"Any man would be lucky to have you, sister, and don't you forget it."

June smiled. "Thank you. I won't. I'd better order your breakfast now."

June picked up the receiver of the room phone and spoke to the cafeteria, then returned it to its cradle and excused herself, finding the visitors lounge at the end of the hall unoccupied.

"Ray?"

"June," he said, sounding surprised.

"Ray, if I were sick, really sick, I mean, would you want to be with me, to take care of me?"

"Of course I would, baby. Why would you even ask a question like that?"

"I don't know. I guess I'm just feeling a little insecure. Thank you for reassuring me. I need to go now. But Ray…"

"What is it, baby?"

"I love you. I mean, I think I'm in love with you."

The silence was deafening.

"I love you, too, baby. And I can't wait to show you how much tonight."

Fifty-two

"**S**AVANNAH?"

"Hi, Momma, where are you?"

"I'm in the car, honey, driving to Ray's house. Can you talk a few minutes?"

"Sure, is everything okay?"

"It's fine. I was just wondering, being there at Duke, do you have any friends who are Black?"

Savannah snorted. "Of course, Momma, how could I not? I mean…why are you asking me such a weird question?"

June laughed, too. She imagined her daughter rolling her eyes.

"I was just wondering. You know, when I was at UNC, I really didn't have any Black girlfriends, and certainly no boyfriends. I don't think it was because I was racist—I hope not, anyway. It was a different time. But now, I've made a friend. She's actually a patient, but she's becoming a real friend. She refers to me as her 'sister', and I love it. Of course, Maria is my best friend here, and she's Latina." June shook her head, hoping she was making sense. "I just realized I never had friends of any race other than White when I was growing up, and…well, now it makes me sad."

"That's because you've learned that skin color doesn't mean anything, Momma. There's no such thing as race—that's a social construct. There's only one *human* race. I'm glad you have a new friend. Tell me about your Black sister."

"I wish I could, but I can't, it's top secret here at the clinic. She's a famous movie star, but she's so funny and down-to-earth. I feel like I could talk to her about anything. She's older than I am, and very beautiful…"

"Well, I'm sorry she's in the hospital, but since she is, she's lucky to have you as her nurse. How's Maria?"

"She's good. She invited Ray and me to have dinner with her and her family, but Ray didn't want to, said he didn't need any new friends. It's funny, now that I think of it, I haven't met any of his friends. Or his family, either, for that matter. But he's looking forward to meeting *you* in a couple of weeks. You're still okay with him coming?"

"Of course, that's fine. And, if you don't mind, Marta is going to join us for a couple of nights. It's a four-hour bus ride from Guadalajara to Puerta Vallarta."

"That's wonderful. I'd like a chance to get to know her better, this time under more favorable circumstances." June could almost feel her daughter cringe. "It's fine, Savannah. That night in October is water under the bridge—I've completely forgotten it."

"Thank you, Momma. I'd better go now. I'm meeting my study group at eight."

"I love you, honey."

"I love you too. Bye-bye."

Fifty-three

June pulled into Ray's driveway and sat with the engine running for a short time. Looking around her, it was hard to see any activity at all in this quiet neighborhood. The large lot sizes, and the mature citrus and palm trees, gave her the impression she was on a large, secluded estate. When she and Ray had made love for the first time, beside the pool, the privacy of her surroundings had seemed delicious. Now, over a month later, the isolation felt slightly eerie.

Suddenly, Ray appeared around the corner of the house, carrying a tool of some sort. June turned the key in the ignition and dropped it into her purse, which was all she had with her. Yesterday, she had transferred enough of her clothes and toiletries to be able to stay the night and get ready for work the next morning.

"Hello," she said, opening her door and smiling up at him.

"Don't keep me waiting; I'm hungry."

"Really…what are we having for dinner?"

"I'm not sure, I haven't thought about that yet."

He tossed whatever it was he held in the direction of a dense flowering shrub, and pulled her roughly toward him, starting to unbutton her blouse before they were even in the house. *Had he started drinking without her?*

"I've missed you, baby," he said, as he pulled her toward the sofa, where two martini glasses sat on the coffee table, one of them empty, the other sweating onto the metal surface. He pushed her down and raised the skirt of her uniform. She had a feeling of panic, the memory of a long ago encounter with a fraternity boy in the back seat of a car during one of her brief breakups with Greg. She had been a scared freshman then; she was a grown woman now. She pushed Ray away.

"I'm pleased you're happy to see me," she said, in what she hoped was a strong but soothing voice. "I need a few minutes to unwind. I'll be right back."

She made her way to what they both referred to as *her* room, and quietly closed the door. She dared not risk Ray hearing the click of the lock, and didn't really feel it necessary, despite her uncomfortable flashback. She just needed to get her wits about her. Stepping into the en suite bathroom, she used the toilet, then ran warm water into the basin and freshened herself. Changing into clean undergarments and a casual knit dress helped her relax, as did dabbing a few drops of lavender essential oil on her wrists and behind her ears. Opening the door, she returned to the great room.

"Now I'm ready to party," she said, smiling. She breathed a sigh of relief. Ray had replaced his empty martini glass with a tall iced tea, and sat waiting for her on the sofa. Had she imagined what just happened, or perhaps over-reacted to it? She thought not; but now, as she sat down beside him, she doubted herself. *Too much on my mind…*

As if reading it, Ray asked, "How's it going with your famous patient?" He stroked her leg. "If you really loved me, you'd tell me who she is." He moved his hand under the skirt of her dress—slowly at first, and then with insistence.

"I do love you," she murmured, feeling the heat of his caress, giving in to the gin's initial effect, and her own desire.

Later, over dinner on the patio—lamb chops that Ray had prepared on the grill, and a huge Greek salad—June leaned forward with her glass of zinfandel and reassured him of her feelings.

"Otherwise," she continued, "I would not have invited you to spend the Christmas holidays with Savannah and me. I'm excited for you to meet her. But what about *your* family? I know your parents have passed, and that you have no siblings, but what about cousins?" *Or friends that are like family.* She recalled the Fourth of July picnic with the Chavez clan. She had no doubt they would include her in their Christmas gathering if she were alone. Maria had, in fact, invited Ray and her for Thanksgiving dinner, after June had made a lame excuse about why they couldn't schedule a dinner party, but he had once again declined to meet her friends.

"It's just me, baby. Me and you, that is."

Fifty-four

TWO days before Christmas, June sat with Ray in the American Airlines boarding area at Sky Harbor, waiting for the plane that would fly them to Puerta Vallarta, in the state of Jalisco, Mexico. Ray had made the arrangements, and they had agreed not to check bags. June went back over what she'd packed –swimsuit, cover-up, sandals, two sundresses, a light wrap for dinner, shorts, tee shirts, walking shoes and a hat. And of course a sexy nighty. Since the evening several weeks back, when she'd been uncomfortable with Ray, he'd given her no more cause for concern. Just her imagination running away with her, she'd concluded. She could hardly wait to see Savannah, and to introduce her daughter to the man—as she'd confided to Maria and Jae—she now thought of as her partner.

Even though the flight was not long, Ray had booked seats in first class, and the gate attendant announced that boarding would soon begin. June studied the other passengers, mostly couples and families on holiday, but a few outliers. One man, in particular, caught her attention. He had fine features and wore his hair in cornrows, with the skin of his scalp tattooed between each braid, and a large diamond earring in his left lobe. He and his male companion, who wasn't nearly as attractive, were dressed in business casual attire—pressed pants, open collars, sports jackets. They both seemed to be on the alert, their eyes surveilling the crowd. *Curious...*

June and Ray were soon buckled into their seats, at which point she sent Savannah one final text, confirming an on-time departure. Her daughter was, she hoped, already in the air, but would read the message when she landed.

Three hours later, as they carried their bags down the exit ramp to board a shuttle to the terminal, they were met with a warm, humid breeze. It reminded June of her beloved North Carolina, a fragrant respite from the dry Arizona air. She had wondered how much faster her skin must be aging in the desert climate and had indulged in as many hydrating moisturizers as her budget allowed. When they entered the cool airport and headed toward customs, she glanced back. There was no sign of the men she had observed.

Fifty-five

"MOMMA!" Savannah ran to embrace her, then offered her hand to Ray. "I've heard so much about you. I'm glad you could join us."

"Likewise, Savannah. Why don't the two of you wait here while I visit the registration desk?"

June and her daughter each filled a plastic cup with iced lemon water from a glass dispenser on the welcome table in the lobby, then walked to the expansive, Saltillo-tile patio that opened to the pool. The sparkling Pacific Ocean stretched beyond. Ray had pestered her about upgrading the modest accommodations June had booked back in November, and after putting up a good fight, she gave in to his insistence. Now, both she and Savannah were his guests. While she appreciated his generosity, at the same time, she realized she had relinquished agency.

Ray returned with two sets of access cards, handing one of them to Savannah. "I'm sorry, the rooms are on opposite sides of the hotel," he said, with apparent chagrin.

June tried to hide her disappointment. "I'm sorry, honey."

Savannah accepted the envelope with a smile. "It's okay, Momma. I'm a big girl. Meet you at the bar down there on the beach in a few?"

June smiled back gratefully. "Yes. In a few."

Thirty minutes later, they sat looking away from the huge beachfront hotel, watching the clear, blue-green waves lap at its long, private, white-sand beach. Ray had ordered his usual Bombay Sapphire martini—up, with olives—while June and Savannah sipped their drinks through straws. The exotic rum and pineapple juice concoctions were served in a hollowed-out coconut shell, complete with an umbrella pick. June had insisted—no, demanded—they report to the bar as soon as possible, changing quickly into her swimsuit and cover-up and donning her flip-flops. Ray had tried to seduce her when she removed her clothes, but she had pulled away, offering an apologetic smile and ignoring his sarcastic comment about her lack of gratitude. She wondered now if her actions would have unpleasant consequences, and tried to shake off the feeling of dread. This trip was, after all, her Christmas gift to Savannah, even though Ray had insisted on paying for it, and she hadn't wanted to leave her daughter waiting.

Afternoon faded to evening, the sun a fiery ball gradually falling below the horizon. After a walk on the beach, Savannah returned to the bar with her sandals in hand. June had ordered a second coconut, and Ray another martini.

"Is there a plan for dinner?" Savannah asked.

June felt her daughter's concern, and answered her with deliberation, trying very hard not to slur her words. "Let's make one," she said. "What are you hungry for?"

Savannah consulted an app on her phone for recommendations, and reported that the resort they were staying at had one of the most highly rated restaurants in the Hotel Zone, touted for its excellent farm-to-table menu. The three decided to return to their rooms for showers and a change of clothes before meeting for the reservation Savannah had made online.

During this brief interlude June did succumb to Ray's advance, allowing him to lead her to their bed and remove her scant clothing. Her body melted into his as he parted her lips. She tasted the gin on his tongue and enjoyed the barely lingering fragrance of the musk aftershave he had applied twelve hours earlier. When they finished making love, she raised up onto one elbow to search his eyes, but they were closed. The light from the torches on the hotel grounds cast enough glow for her to see his face clearly in the dark room. She was struck by the realization that she knew very little about the man lying next to her, a man she had allowed herself to become intimate with and increasingly dependent on.

A chill crept down her spine. She rolled over onto her back and pulled the covers up to her chin, contemplating her options. Of the ones she considered, slowing the pace of their developing relationship made the most sense, and she resolved to do so when they returned home. Decision made, she got up to shower.

Fifty-six

FRANK and Margaret were running errands in Fountain Hills on Christmas Eve day. This was an annual tradition for the two of them—one they both looked forward to. This year, they were out purchasing last minute stocking stuffers for the girls, picking up their order of red chili pork and green chili corn tamales from their favorite taqueria, and selecting a small turkey and a bottle of sparkling wine at Safeway. Maria was bringing a friend to dinner that night. As was their custom, both Frank and his sister had volunteered to work on Christmas Day to give their colleagues time with family visiting from out-of-town.

As Margaret emptied their cart of its few contents, sending them on the conveyer belt toward the cashier, the store manager approached Frank, urgently pulling him aside.

"Honey, you go ahead and finish checking out. Tom needs me outside for a minute."

Margaret waved him off with a smile. They had been married long enough, he knew, for her to be used to this kind of interruption.

The store manager filled Frank in on what was happening as they walked to the outskirts of the parking lot. They approached a woman who stood at the open back door of an older model vehicle with Tennessee license plates. Frank could make out three tow-headed children waiting in the car, the youngest crying, and the oldest, a boy, trying to sooth her. The car was otherwise packed with what appeared to be bedding and clothes.

"Excuse me, ma'am," Frank said, "I'm afraid you forgot to pay for your groceries. Tom, here, is concerned about it, and asked if I could help. I'm the deputy sheriff here in Fountain Hills."

The woman, who was dressed in a thin sweater and worn-out tennis shoes, looked at the two men with resignation, a tear slipping down her cheek.

"I didn't mean no harm, sir. It ain't much—just some sliced turkey and some bread, and three apples. I just wanted to have something special for my kids for Christmas."

Frank nodded sympathetically. "Where are you and your children staying?"

"We got nowhere to stay but this car. We're on our way to California. I have a brother there who said he'd take us in while I get back on my feet. I just got out of prison in Nashville, got my kids out of foster care, and I'm making my way out there. But coming across New Mexico, the weather slowed us down, and I ran out of money. I'm sorry, but I didn't know what else to do." She looked at the children, then back at the men. "My babies are hungry."

Frank thought about his own two girls at home, eagerly awaiting his return and the start of the family festivities—about the tree, and the presents piled high beneath it. He pulled his phone out of his pocket and stepped aside. "Just give me a minute, and we'll see what we can do to help."

To the manager he said, "I'll take it from here, Tom. Please let my wife know I'll meet her at the car in a few minutes. Here are the keys, so she can let herself in."

Tom returned to the store while Frank called La Casita, a resource center for people experiencing homelessness in the Fountain Hills area. After arranging a short stay for the woman and her children, he led her back into the store and found the manager.

"Tom, this is Marlene. She and her children are going to spend a couple of nights at La Casita before continuing their travels. I've told her to pick out some groceries for their stay, and to fill her tank with gas. I'll cover the costs."

A relieved expression crossed the store manager's face. "Fine," he said, "thanks, Sheriff." Frank nodded.

"Good luck with your travels, ma'am. Give us a holler and let us know you made it safely to your brother's," Frank said, handing Marlene a card with his contact information. "And a Merry Christmas to you and your family."

Fifty-seven

"*FELIZ Navidad, Hermano,*" Maria said to Frank, as she entered the house. The cozy living room was a bustle of activity as Scottie and Ginny hastily finished wrapping gifts that would soon be opened.

"Meet Tony Block, one of your buddies from over in Carefree. Tony and I are taking a class together at Harrington House."

"Come in, come in," Frank said, disguising his surprise, noting his sister's scarlet cheeks. *She's been holding out on me.* "Carefree, eh? How's my old classmate Trevor Smith getting along?"

"He's good," Tony said, shaking Frank's hand. "Nice home you have here. Thank you for including me in your holiday celebration."

"The more the merrier," Frank said. He wanted to ask if there was anything new in the Rancho Manana murder investigation—which seemed to have gone cold, based on what little he knew—but refrained from saying anything in front of the twins and his mother. And, it was Christmas Eve, after all.

Margaret came around the corner smiling, her hand extended, her cheeks flushed from her activity in the kitchen. Sweet and savory aromas wafted in her wake, and in that moment, Frank felt, as he often did, that he was the luckiest man alive.

While Maria went directly to their dozing mother and planted a kiss on top of her bobbing head, Frank went to the kitchen, returning with two open beer bottles. His girls looked up at the visitor with twin looks of curiosity, then returned to their last-minute preparations.

Frank invited Tony to sit, and after a bit of small talk, gave in to his urge to know more about the murder.

"Fact is," Tony said, "we're sort of at a dead end, no pun intended." He gave a self-conscious laugh. "I made a trip up to Nevada, where the victim had lived and worked. Lots of folks there who had good reason to be unhappy about him getting out early to go and sit by a pool at a golf resort—I heard some stories for sure. Talked to his ex-wife. Since then, I've talked to his kids. But I didn't talk to anyone who seemed to want him dead bad enough to kill him."

He'd lowered his voice as he spoke the last words and Frank signaled his appreciation.

"We don't even know what he was doing in our area."

Not my district, not my problem. Still, Frank was intrigued.

"Frank?" Margaret called from the kitchen, and he excused himself to join her.

"Do you plan to carve the turkey in here, or at the table?" she asked over her shoulder as she washed her hands.

"Hmmm, you smell good," he said, kissing her lightly under a sprig of mistletoe he had hung strategically above the sink. "I'm conflicted. It's easier in the kitchen. But the dining room table makes us look more like a Norman Rockwell family."

"You have to be the only sheriff in Arizona who even knows who Norman Rockwell is! And, you'd have to go put on a suit and tie if that's the look you're after." They both laughed, as Frank covered his jeans and plaid Western shirt with an apron bearing the imprint *Don't Worry, I Can do This—I Watched a YouTube Video.* He picked up a ten-inch butcher's knife and addressed the bird.

"Girls, time to fill the water glasses. Dinner in ten minutes," Margaret said, in the direction of the living room.

Maria, with Tony's help, escorted Aurelia into the dining room and seated her in her special place at the table. Once they were all gathered, Frank asked them to hold hands while he offered his traditional blessing.

"*Señor Dios, Padre celestial: Bendícenos y bendice estos tus dones, que de tu gran bondad recibimos. Por Jesucristo, nuestro Señor.*"

"Amen," everyone responded.

"Cheers," Frank said, raising his water glass and toasting his 'girls'—as he like to call the five females in his family—and their guest.

Maria's phone vibrated on the table, and she smiled apologetically. "On call," she explained, excusing herself from the table and heading down the hall to Aurelia's room for privacy.

"So, Tony, how long have you been with District Four?" Frank asked, serving his mother, who sat to his left, an especially tender slice of turkey breast which he had set aside just for her. He judged Tony to be five or six years younger than himself, somewhere around thirty-five.

"Five years," Tony said, accepting the sweet potato casserole Margaret passed. "Prior to that I was with Coconino County, up in Flagstaff."

"Flagstaff!" said Ginny. "I've heard they have snow up there."

"Sometimes they do." Tony smiled at both girls. "Do you like snow?"

"We've never seen it," they said in unison. "Except on the top of Four Peaks," added Scottie.

"They've led sheltered lives," Margaret said, laughing. "Maybe we should take a drive up north over the holiday, Frank, and let the girls build a snowman."

Maria slipped back into her chair just in time to receive the cranberry sauce as it came around. "Sorry."

"No worries, Sis. Everything okay?"

"Sure…just a couple of questions that came up with the night staff," she said, but Frank could see she was distracted during the topics of conversation that ensued—how perfectly Margaret had roasted the turkey, how spicy the tamales were this year, and the possibility of a road trip sometime during the next few days.

After he was more than full of his wife's wonderful cooking, Frank offered to clean up.

"You wash, and I'll dry. Just like the old days," his sister said.

"You seemed worried, is everything okay?" Frank asked, while the sink filled with hot, soapy water. "By the way, Tony seems like a good egg." Maria hadn't had many boyfriends—as lovely as she was—and he'd never bonded with any of them.

"Yes, he is," she nodded. "But I *am* worried. That was Savannah calling me."

"Savannah?" The name was familiar, but he couldn't quite place it.

"June's daughter."

"Oh, yeah, I remember. But, why was she calling *you*?"

"She's worried about her mother and she wondered if I shared her concerns."

"And?"

"And I told her I did. I've been concerned about June for weeks, but I haven't known what to do, other than be there for her if she decides she wants to talk about it."

"What are you two doing in here, anyway? Come out to the living room and play charades with us. Then I'll serve some pie. And the girls would like you to open the present they made for you." Margaret put her arm around her sister-in-law and guided her toward the living room. Maria turned back toward Frank, and tossed him her towel. Unless he was mistaken, which he doubted, he glimpsed something akin to fear in her eyes.

Fifty-eight

"YOUR family is amazing," said Tony, as he walked Maria to her door. "Thank you for including me tonight. I know you have work tomorrow, but I was thinking we might catch a movie after you get off. We could have dinner, too, if we can find anything open that late on Christmas."

"That sounds nice, Tony, thank you. I'd like to say 'yes' right now, but something has come up. May I let you know later in the day? I hope that doesn't sound rude."

"No problem. As of now, I'm not doing anything tomorrow except maybe taking a mountain hike with Rusty. Why don't you call me whenever it's convenient?"

Maria knew that Tony had recently acquired a dog—part German Shepherd and part Husky, an older dog, he had said, fully trained. He had proudly shown her a picture of the handsome animal wearing a bandana around his thick, muscular neck. She had never owned a dog, and Tony's excitement about his new canine companion made her smile.

"Good. We have a plan. And Tony, Merry Christmas." She kissed him lightly on the cheek and slipped inside.

Fifty-nine

MARGARET rested her head on Frank's shoulder, and he pulled her close. They sat on a love seat that was a little small for a man of his height, in front of a new kiva fireplace in the corner of their living room, its ambiance and warmth encircling them. It was his Christmas gift to his wife, installed the week after Thanksgiving, and had become their favorite place to unwind together after the other members of the household had retired to their rooms.

"So, I can't stop thinking about that woman at Safeway," Margaret said. "I hope she and her children are okay."

"Me too." He lifted her chin and kissed her tenderly.

"And what was going on with Maria tonight? Was it really the clinic calling her on Christmas Eve? I mean, I know her job is essential..."

"It wasn't the clinic. It was June's daughter. The two are spending the holidays in Mexico, with June's boyfriend. Savannah's worried about her mother and called Maria. That's all I know."

"Hmm, that's troubling. I wonder if there's anything we can do to help."

Frank was already wracking his brain for ideas, but without having any solid information he was coming up empty.

"I'll call Maria tomorrow and ask. But for now, I just want to enjoy being here with my sweetheart." He kissed Margaret again, this time more deeply. He had met her their freshman year, at the university, in Tucson, on a blind date. They married after graduation, then moved Frank's mother and his younger sister from the Chicago area to Arizona. That was over fifteen years ago. Margaret was the only woman Frank had ever loved—or made love to. He planned to keep it that way.

Sixty

MARIA entered Jae's room quietly, but the famous actor was sitting up in bed, talking on her cell phone, laughing. Maria could overhear the voices of an older woman, and a man. June had told her that Jae's only close family members were her mother—who suffered too many health problems to travel—and a brother, who was their mother's caregiver. For that reason, Jae would be alone in the hospital with no one visiting over the holidays. It was one of the reasons Maria, who had seniority, had volunteered to work on Christmas Day. That, and the fact that she wanted to give the nurses with children the day off.

Christmas is, after all, for children. Maria had not given much thought to having children, since she had never met anyone she wanted to have them with. But lately, she was aware that her biological clock was ticking. If she wanted to conceive and bear children, there wasn't much time left for her to get started. She knew of women who had adopted as single parents, and even women who had frozen their eggs for later implantation. And, of course, there was IVF, but…

Maria had what she knew were pretty traditional ideas about the progression of love, followed by marriage, and, only then, the proverbial baby carriage. She and Frank had teased each other with that silly rhyme growing up any time one or the other of them seemed to be attracted to a member of the opposite sex. If only she could find someone to be as happy with as her brother was with Margaret.

As if on cue, her phone vibrated, and she saw that it was Frank. She gave a little wave to Jae and mouthed "I'll be back" as she exited the room.

"Feliz Navidad," she answered.

"Merry Christmas to you, too, Sis. I wanted to follow up with you about June. What's going on?"

"Savannah sounded pretty upset, said she didn't know who else to call. I'm not sure how she got my number—her mother's phone contacts, probably. She said her mother was drinking way too much. She said Ray checked all three of them in, and that their room and hers are on opposite ends of this big resort. He told them that was what the hotel had available, but when Savannah casually mentioned it to someone at the front desk a day later, she was assured they could have been assigned rooms right next to each other. She said Ray seems to be dominating her mother, and that June acts like a zombie."

"That doesn't sound like the June we know, does it? I mean, she's had a streak of bad luck, but she isn't out of it. Have you met this guy, Ray?"

"No. In fact, I don't even know his last name. Given June's history with men, he may be bad news. But she was so sure he was different, and I was hopeful. Anyway, they aren't due to return until the thirtieth. Savannah wasn't sure she could take it that long, but her friend, Marta, is coming tomorrow for two days, so she has to hold out until then. I promised to call her this morning—I thought maybe things would seem better in the light of day. I even had the thought last night of flying down there, but that's not practical. And what could I do? It must be hard for Savannah, seeing her mother with a man who isn't her dad."

"Well, let me know. Hopefully you and I will both have quiet, uneventful days. *Adios.*"

"*Adios, Hermano.*"

Sixty-one

"TONY?"

"Merry Christmas, Maria. What's the verdict? Dinner and a movie?"

"Yes, please. Shall I meet you somewhere?"

"We can do that—there's a dine-in option in the theater at Talking Stick. They have some new holiday releases. Or, if you aren't put off by a somewhat shabby bachelor pad and a little dog hair, I picked up a frozen pizza and a salad last night on my way home. We could open a bottle of wine and watch a movie here. I have a big screen, mostly for sports, you know. And you could meet Rusty."

Maria laughed. She didn't know Tony well—yet—but she was sure she knew his preference for the evening. "I'm off at five. I'll change into some jeans here and drive straight to your place. Text me your address."

"Great. I think it will take you about thirty-five minutes to get here. See you soon."

At exactly five-forty-five, Maria rang the doorbell at Tony Block's apartment in the Pinnacle Peak area near Carefree, the town where the District Four office he reported to most days was located. The building was an older one—eighties vintage, she guessed—but well-maintained. Tony opened the door wide, and she could see beyond into his small but neat living room, with its out-of-proportion-sized flat screen monitor mounted on the wall opposite the sofa.

A big dog loped over to greet her, alternately yelping with pleasure as she leaned down to scratch his ears, and licking her ankles with enthusiasm. This was, explained Tony, both a greeting and a compliment. As she and Rusty continued to make friends with each other, Maria took in the apartment. The furniture was sparse, but adequate. All the upholstery was some variation of brown, but there were colorful desert touches—turquoise, orange, and lime green throw pillows, and a pair of framed posters—photos of nebulae taken from the Kitt Peak National Observatory in Tucson.

All in all, it was charming. She nodded her approval at Tony, who beamed his gratitude in return.

"May I pour you a glass of wine?" he asked. "Rusty, stop licking!" he scolded.

"Please," she laughed. "I need one." As Tony took two glasses from a cabinet and poured a few ounces of red wine into each, Maria continued to take in her surroundings. For the first time, she noticed a small, artificial Christmas tree on a table in the corner, a colorful cloth draped around its base. After accepting a stemmed glass from Tony, she walked closer to the tree, and saw that it was decorated with a collection of mis-matched glass balls and a few children's ornaments, including a little bear holding a sign that said "Baby's First Xmas", a stuffed felt elf, and a star Santa created from popsicle sticks, red construction paper, and small, white cotton pom-poms.

"Tell me about this one," she said, pointing at the ornament clearly made by a young child.

"I will, if you tell me why you need that glass of wine." He winked at her and walked over to where she was standing. "Okay, I'll go first. As you know, my mother died when I was five. She loved children—she used to invite all the neighborhood kids to our house around the holidays, to bake cookies and make ornaments. This is one I made the Christmas before she died, so it's special to me. You've heard that old question, 'if your house was on fire, what would you take?' I'd probably grab the box with the tree trimmings." He led her toward the sofa, seating himself a respectable distance from her. "Your turn."

"I'm not sure where to start. That call I got last night was from the daughter of a friend. Mother and daughter are spending the week in Mexico, and the daughter is concerned her mother is drinking too much and giving in too often to her man-friend, who's there with them. You know how Camille talked in one of our sessions about depersonalization disorder, and how abuse could sometimes bring that on? My friend suffered physical abuse in her first marriage, and now she may be experiencing emotional abuse. I'm not sure how to approach her about it, or if I even should.

"She has a special patient assigned to her at the clinic, and it's clear they've become close, though we discourage that. Anyway, I'm covering for her, and this patient told me today that she has seen changes in my friend's level of confidence, within a short period of time. So, now it's become a professional issue as well." Maria paused, feeling suddenly overwhelmed.

Tony moved closer, tentatively putting his arm around her shoulder. "May I?" he asked.

Maria leaned into his muscular bicep, relaxing and breathing a small sigh of release. They sat like this, neither speaking, until Rusty rushed into the room carrying a plush rattlesnake in his mouth and laid the dog-toy at Maria's feet, commencing to lick her ankles again.

"Oh, Rusty," they said in unison, laughing and ruffling the fur on the animal's neck.

"I see your dilemma," Tony said. "Let me pre-heat the oven and we can talk some more. Or, if you'd like a break from thinking about it, we can see what's available to watch."

"The latter, I think. And a little more wine, please."

He returned with the bottle and the remote, and proceeded to scroll through the network and cable offerings, apologizing that he didn't subscribe to any streaming services. There was an assortment of holiday themed movies, old and new, and they narrowed it down to a choice between *Love Actually*, and *Christmas with the Kranks*. Tony said the movies sounded familiar, but he couldn't remember anything about either one. Maria liked them both but decided the lighter, more ridiculous Kranks—played by Tim Allen and Jamie Lee Curtis—were a better antidote to her mood.

In between salad, pepperoni pizza and more wine they laughed their way through three hours of silliness and commercials, and when Maria said she'd better leave if she intended to get to work on time in the morning, it was with reluctance. Tony walked her to her car, and waited, shivering in the chilly night air, as she turned the key in the ignition. Impulsively, she lowered her window, and raised her lips for him to kiss goodnight, which he did, lingering.

"Maria?" he said.

"Yes?" She could see his breath.

"This has been the best Christmas of my life."

Sixty-two

SAVANNAH, and her friend Marta, who had arrived from Guadalajara that morning, were strolling the square that defined La Isla Puerto Vallarta, a modern outdoor shopping mall in the hotel zone not far from where they were staying. They sat down on a stone bench to enjoy the fountains, and watched as an old woman, a once colorful but now faded *rebozo* draped around her shoulders, massaged a coin between the thumb and two forefingers of her right hand before tossing it into the pool nearest them. Surrounding the water features were tropical gardens—birds-of-paradise and bougainvillea. Peacocks strolled among the shoppers, preening their elongated tail feathers and crying their cat calls.

"Such a lovely scene," said Savannah. "If only..."

"What's going on, *Amiga, dime*..."

"I wish I knew. My mom has this boyfriend—that sounds so stupid when you're talking about people their age—and he seems to be gaslighting her. His name is Ray, Ray Prentice.

"He's handsome, I guess, for someone as old as he is, and he has good manners, which is important to my mom. But he's dominating, and he's constantly ordering cocktails for her. You know how small she is, she can't handle that much alcohol. She's never been a drinker—an occasional glass of wine, maybe." Savannah felt herself getting worked up and stopped talking, breathing deeply before continuing.

"Anyway, I'm glad you're here. I called my mother's friend, Maria, in Scottsdale, on Christmas Eve. She checked back in with me the next day—even offered to fly down here if I needed her to—but I started wondering if it was all in my head. I think he's gaslighting us both. And now, I don't know, I think they may be getting married…"

"*Qué lástima*, I'm so sorry. Your mother is sweet. And the fact that she was in favor of my coming here after the incident last October—I'm still embarrassed."

"Me too. But that blunder—that was my fault, not yours. Momma's always been afraid of losing me. I need to be more sensitive. But right now, I'm the one's who's afraid—of losing *her*."

Sixty-three

"WELL, well, what have we here?" Jae sat upright in a recliner in her room at the Mayo, eating whole-wheat toast and an omelet from the flowered plate on the tray June had pulled over to her.

"Black-eyed peas," said June. "It's a New Year's Day tradition, you know. I asked the chef to add a small bowl to your breakfast tray. But you only need to eat a spoonful for a year's worth of good luck." She smiled encouragingly. According to the reports she had reviewed when she arrived at the clinic this morning at six, Jae would need not only good luck but divine intervention to conquer her disease.

"I was referring to the rock on your finger, sister. Did you become engaged over the Christmas holiday?"

"I…I'm not sure."

Jae gave her a quizzical look, and she shrugged her shoulders.

Ray had presented her with a small, gift-wrapped box on Christmas morning as she sipped the cup of coffee he had placed on her bedside table. She had smiled at him as she pulled the red satin ribbon, slowly untying it, and then removing the shiny silver paper that revealed a white jeweler's gift box. Nestled inside it was a red velvet box. She had simply stared at it.

"Well, aren't you going to open it?"

June had felt paralyzed. Finally she'd removed the smaller box from the larger one, and—taking a deep breath—opened it. The emerald-cut blue sapphire, set in white gold and guarded by two diamond baguettes, was stunning in its beauty and simplicity. She had never owned anything so exquisite. Even the sophisticated dinner rings her wealthy grandmother had passed down to her mother, who had passed them on to her, paled by comparison. It was the most beautiful piece of jewelry she had ever seen. She looked up at Ray, tears in her eyes.

"Thank you."

"You're welcome, baby. Merry Christmas." He pulled the ring from the white satin cushion that held it in place and slid it onto the ring finger of her left hand. Then he gently removed the nightgown she was wearing, and just as gently made love to her.

Later that morning, at breakfast, with Savannah, June shyly and silently displayed her left hand for her daughter to admire, which she did, looking from her mother to Ray for the answer to the obvious question. Ray only smiled, and June wasn't sure what the answer was, so she said nothing. And now, a week later, she still wasn't sure of the true significance of the ring. In the absence of a proposal, she had to take it for a beautiful and extravagant gift, and in a way that was a huge relief.

Sixty-four

THAT night at dinner Ray spoke the words June had been dreading.

"I'd like you to move your things to my place, Junie—start the new year out right here with me. I've arranged for a company that will pack them up for you while you're at work."

"But Ray, I'm here already. I mean, I'm here every night. And my place is so much closer to the clinic." She tried to give him her most convincing smile.

"But, to your point, you're here every night. So, it just makes sense for your things to be here with you. As it is now, your place is just a big closet. Trust me, June, I have your best interest in mind."

His voice sounded condescending, and June felt suffocated. She forced herself to breathe. He couldn't just move her things, could he? When he had asked for a key to her apartment, he had said it was so he could check on her if there was ever a problem. He had sounded concerned, and the request had seemed like a thoughtful idea. Had he, by any chance, entered her apartment without her knowing? The thought chilled her, although she had nothing to hide. She tried another argument.

"Ray, I have friends, the Chavez family, the ones I want you to meet? My place is closer to where they live. And I like doing things in Fountain Hills, even though I haven't lately, that is, since you and I have been together."

"I understand. And you can still see your friend Maria at work, right?"

"Right, but…"

"June, we don't need to keep rehashing this. I want you here with me, that's all. Let's celebrate with another drink, shall we?"

Sixty-five

"**I'M** trapped," June said. She had held it in for as long as she could. She sensed that her good friend knew that things were not okay, and she finally felt ready to admit it.

"Tell me more." Maria said. The two sat in a corner of the hospital cafeteria during their thirty-minute lunch break.

"Ray's moving my things to his place and closing mine down."

"Wait a minute, don't you have a lease?"

"He contacted my landlord and arranged to pay the early termination fee."

"June, your boyfriend, fiancé, whatever he is, can't just move you without your consent."

"I tried to tell him that."

"June, this is serious. This man is taking control of your life and you're allowing it. Do you love him?"

"I'm not sure. I thought I did. And I think—thought— he loved me."

"June, controlling another person is not a loving thing to do. Look, I'm not sure about the excuses you've given for why Ray doesn't want to get together socially with me and my family. Maybe they're valid. But it appears to me that he's trying to isolate you, and make you question your own judgement. That's emotional abuse. Who knows what he'll do next—tell you that your job isn't important, and that he wants you to stay home every day?"

June stared down at her plate. She had no appetite. She hadn't felt like eating lately. Her clothes were starting to feel a little loose, and not in a good way. She wasn't sleeping well, and when she looked in the mirror, she thought her face seemed more lined, her skin sallow.

"I'd better go check on Jae," she said.

Maria nodded, and reached out to touch June's hand. "It's always hard to say 'goodbye' to a special patient. I'm so sorry it's coming on top of this situation with Ray."

Sixty-six

"FRANK?"

"*Hola, Maria, ¿que pasa?*"

"Guess."

"June?"

"She's in trouble, Frank."

He could tell by the gravitas in his sister's voice that this was no time to poke fun at the predicaments their friend was known for getting into. In fact, he and Margaret had been revisiting their mutual concern for June ever since her daughter had called Maria on Christmas Eve. The fact that she had continued to make excuses for not getting together with them was puzzling to Margaret, and Frank found it concerning as well.

"Say more."

"This relationship she's been in since October has turned sinister. Her boyfriend's now insisting she move in with him. He told her he's arranged for movers to come and pack up her apartment this weekend, despite her protests. The instructor in that course that Tony and I took? She called this type of behavior 'coercive control'.

"Oh, and he gave her this gorgeous ring for Christmas. It looks like an engagement ring, but he hasn't asked her to marry him. She thought she was in love with him—now she isn't so sure. But the ring is making her feel obligated. I think she's scared. And maybe embarrassed, poor thing."

"What's this guy's name?"

"Ray Prentice. I don't know much about him, but I'll tell you what I know. What are you planning to do?"

"I'm not sure."

Sixty-seven

"NANCY?"

"Frank! How've you been? Any news about that murder? I think about it all the time. So disturbing! How's Margaret? How's your mother? How're the twins?

Frank, sitting at his office desk, laughed out loud. Nancy Scott was a force unto herself, a powerhouse like no one he had ever encountered. He could see her freckled face and her mass of short red curls across the wire. He grew more confident about his plan.

"Everyone's fine, Detective. And Ben? And the Crouches?" Two could play her game.

"All good. You're giving me that moniker again. What's up?"

"I need your help. But let's not discuss it over the phone. Are you free for lunch?"

"You bet! The usual venue? Noon?"

"See you then."

Sixty-eight

FRANK settled into a red vinyl booth at Phil's Filling Station and waited for his friend to come bursting through the door, which she did momentarily. Nancy was often out of breath and today was no exception. He stood to shake her hand. He really liked this woman and, what was more, he respected her immensely.

"Sorry I'm late!" she said, sliding in across from him.

"No problem. Thanks for meeting me. Let's order, and then we can get down to business."

They placed their orders for burgers, fries, and Cokes—diet for Frank—then leaned across the table conspiratorially.

"I'll get right to the point. My sister has a good friend, a nurse at the clinic. She's become a friend of Margaret's and mine as well. Her name is June Lambreth."

"That name sounds familiar—I think I've met her! Go on."

"June is in a relationship with a man that Maria thinks is bad news. We don't know anything about him, although we've tried to meet him. I can't really afford to use the resources of the department to investigate him, especially since there's been no complaint. I ran a background check but came up empty-handed. I thought maybe you'd be willing to do a little sleuthing, with the understanding that if you come across something that doesn't feel right, you bring me into the loop right away. I don't want you going rogue..." He could see the excitement in Nancy's eyes.

"I'm on it, Frank! What's the guy's name?"

"Ray Prentice, P-R-E-N-T-I-C-E. Assuming it's Raymond. Lives in Scottsdale. June spends every night with him these days, and he's arranged to have her stuff moved there, later this week, against her will. All Maria knows about the guy is that he was—maybe still is—in medical billing services, and that he has a lot of money. Sorry, I know it's not much to go on."

"No worries, you know I love a challenge! I'll let you know as soon as I have anything. Did you say the movers are coming this week?"

"Saturday."

"Shit. Okay, let's get going, as soon as we finish these burgers."

Sixty-nine

TREVOR Smith was sitting with his deputies, Jack Powell and Tony Block, at the First Watch on North Scottsdale Road. "So, fellas, we need to double down on this Hamilton thing. Just because no one seems to care that he's dead doesn't mean we don't have to solve his murder."

Jack guffawed.

"What's so damned funny?" Trevor asked.

"Nothing, sorry. That just reminds me of the Dixie Chicks song about the guy who abuses his wife, then she and her girlfriend poison him and dump him in the lake. The 'missing person that nobody missed at all'? Cindy loves that song." Jack grinned. "By the way, we're getting married."

"No kidding!" Tony said. "What'd you do to change her mind?"

"I convinced her that if I *did* die in the line of duty, which has been her big fear, she'd be better off getting my survivor benefits than she would be getting zilch. I guess money really does talk. She saw the logic."

"Well congrats. I'm happy for you," Tony said.

"Likewise," Trevor said, "that's great. Now, back to business. A murder was committed in our backyard over two months ago and we still have no idea who did it. As my buddy Frank Chavez likes to say, 'somebody knows something', and my money is on the wife. Block, I think there's another trip back to Vegas in your future. Spend the night and take in a show."

"Got it. Maybe I'll invite my girlfriend to go with me."

"Girlfriend?" Jack said.

"I thought you got a dog," Trevor said.

"I did," Tony said, "and then I got lucky and met a girl. So, now I have a dog *and* a girlfriend. Actually, at this point, she's a friend, who's a girl. But I'm hopeful." He didn't mention that Maria was the younger sister of Frank Chavez, who inspired both admiration and envy from his professional colleagues.

"Well, good luck with that. Take her to Las Vegas with you, and, who knows? Stay at a decent hotel; I'll approve it."

"Thanks."

Seventy

NANCY Scott waited in the tastefully appointed reception area of Vi at Grayhawk for one of its residents, Charles McBride, whom she had called only last night. Mr. McBride was quite friendly, and had insisted she come over this morning, inviting her to stay for lunch. She had declined the luncheon invitation, but now felt a twinge of regret. The dining room, which she could glimpse from where she sat, was white-tablecloth elegant, and its flavorful smells made her salivate. She should have eaten a bigger breakfast, but she had been in a hurry to hit the road. Scottsdale traffic could be a nightmare. Today, however, there were no accidents or work crews to slow her down, and she had arrived ten minutes early, giving her a chance to take in the surroundings.

She was familiar with continuing care retirement communities, CCRCs as they were called, from her mother's friends, who lived in various places, and from some work Ben had done on a place south of Denver, in Highlands Ranch. But this one topped anything she had seen. It was more like a resort. The woman at the front desk, who looked like a model, greeted her warmly and offered to bring her a cup of coffee, which she accepted. Now, smartly dressed seniors passed through the lobby, no doubt ready to embark on their choice of the day's activities posted on a nearby kiosk—golf, bridge, a lecture, or a museum outing. Everyone nodded and smiled.

If she understood the concept, these residents had sold their homes, bought one of the various models at Vi, and planned to be here for the rest of their lives, accessing progressive levels of assistance as needed, some eventually moving to the memory care unit. And from what her mother had said, the social activities and shared meals resulted in a longer lifespan than the traditional aging in place in one's home. It sounded great, but it looked very expensive.

"Ms. Scott?"

Startled from her thoughts, Nancy looked up at a gentleman in his mid-eighties, his skin a healthy tan, his salt-and-pepper hair combed back in a distinguished style, his hand extended. She jumped to her feet to shake it, taking in the scent of his after-shave and admiring the crispness of his button-down collared shirt. She was glad she had worn her best shoes and her most professional skirt and jacket.

"Mr. McBride, thank you so much for agreeing to meet me, and on such short notice."

He motioned her to sit down and sat next to her.

"Of course, happy to do it. And please, call me Charlie, every-one does. May I call you Nancy?"

"Yes, of course."

"I hope I can be of assistance. As I understand it, you've already published one book, a murder mystery. I did a little detective work of my own." His blue eyes twinkled when he smiled. He was still very handsome.

"That's right. The book I'm working on now is also a mystery, and one of my characters owns a medical billing service. In looking through some old copies of the *Phoenix Business Journal,* I saw that you sold a very successful company, and I wanted to understand more about the inner workings of that kind of business."

"I see. Well, that sale took place over twenty years ago, and I'm sure things have changed, what with hospitals buying up medical practices, and hedge funds buying up hospitals, and all. But it's a lucrative business, at least mine was. That is, until the dot-com bust."

Nancy nodded, then segued to her real interest. "The man you sold it to, Ray Prentiss, he was an employee?"

"That's right, although I thought of him more as a junior partner. Brilliant fellow—came to work for me right out of college. He started out in the call center and quickly worked his way up. By the time of the slowdown, he was my CFO—chief financial officer. He delivered the bad news to me, told me we were losing money hand over foot. He offered up a menu of strategies to stop the bleeding. But while I was still considering them, Ray offered to buy me out. I had had a good run of it—put aside a lot of money when things were good, then inherited a nice portfolio when my dad passed—so I decided to let him have a go of it."

"You *gave* him the business?"

"No, I didn't mean it that way. But in hindsight, I practically gave it to him. And from what I've heard, he made quite a turnaround. We didn't really stay in touch. My wife became ill, and we moved here, so she could get the care she needed. She passed ten years ago."

"I'm sorry," Nancy, said, then persisted. "This brilliant fellow, Ray, who bought your business, what was his background?"

"Average middle-class upbringing, I think, worked his way through college as an EMT. That actually came in handy one time. He resuscitated one of our employees when she suffered a heart attack at her desk."

"Wife, kids?"

"Neither, to my knowledge. Ray was a good-looking guy, but he didn't seem to have much of a social life. Not that I would have known; he kept that to himself, just like I kept Betsy's illness to myself. He was charming—that's the word. Before he stepped into the executive role, he exhibited great people skills with our various constituents, especially when a situation had to be escalated.

"He was good with the patients, who called in to question how their claims were being handled. He was good with the docs—or with their practice managers—who pressed us for better collections. And he was good with the commercial insurance companies and the Medicare folks—they're the ones who really run the show. Yes, charming is the word I'd use for Ray. But if charm didn't work, he was steely, determined. Ray knew how to get things done."

Seventy-one

"HEY, Nancy, what'd you find out?" Frank spoke into his smartphone.

"Nothing too ominous. Ray went to work for Med-Cap Billing Solutions right out of college, late eighties. He was a whiz kid, worked his way up from customer service to the C-suite within a few years, bought the company at a discount from its founder and president when the economy turned south in 2000. He then bought up similar firms that were struggling, had himself a little empire. Interesting tidbit—at least to me, and I'm no business major—rather than sell the company off to some conglomerate when he decided to retire, he simply closed the door."

"Odd."

"The spelling of his last name is P-R-E-N-T-I-S-S, not the other way. And a bit of trivia, he worked his way through school as an emergency medical technician. I'm sorry I don't have more— no skeletons in his closet that I could find. House is fully paid for, property taxes around ten grand a year. Nice big lot, quiet neighborhood, I drove by. Hard to see anything from the street. Ray Prentiss has kept a low profile, literally and figuratively."

Seventy-two

"**M**ARIA?"

"Hi, Tony." Her voice sounded strained. Was it because she was at work, or was she feeling shy about that kiss? Whichever, the sound of her voice speaking his name sent a wave of excitement coursing through his body.

"Can you talk for a few minutes?"

"Only a few," she said in a whisper, which confirmed his first impression.

"Okay, I'll be brief. I have to fly to Las Vegas for an interview tomorrow. Boss told me to spend the night and take in a show. I checked, and I can get two tickets to see the Eagles, at the Sphere. Can you take off work and go with me?"

Silence.

"What's the Sphere?"

Was she stalling?

"Great venue for concerts, and I've heard this one is really good."

"I've never been to Las Vegas," she said.

"No kidding! Then you have to say 'yes,'" he urged.

"It isn't a good time for me to take off, Tony, a combination of things…"

"When's the last time you did something special for yourself, Maria?" He wondered if he was being unfair, trying to guilt her. After all, she was a grown woman, highly competent. He respected her, and knew he should encourage her to do what she felt was right. But he really wanted her with him.

"Where would we be staying?" Was this her real concern?

"I haven't gotten that far. But if you say 'yes,' I'll reserve two rooms for us somewhere on the Strip." No way was he going to try to seduce Frank Chavez's sister in a hotel room in Vegas. "You won't believe the lights, twenty-four, seven. It's a fun place, for a night. Great food, too." He was selling now, his desire for her company increasing as he laid out the benefits of a getaway together.

"Let me think about it, just for an hour. Is that okay? I need to check in on everything here. And Tony?"

"Yes?"

"Thank you for the invitation. It really does sound fun."

Seventy-three

FOR the second time, Tony rang the doorbell of Margie Johnson's condominium on East Tropicana, and waited for her to let him in. She hadn't sounded surprised when he called.

"Hello again," he said, when she opened the door. Today she was wearing a lightweight pink sweatshirt with cranberry-colored embroidery around the shoulders, flared light-blue denim jeans, and flip-flops. Her shoulder-length brown hair was tucked behind her ears, which sported diamond studs, large ones that Tony suspected were the real deal. She didn't appear to be wearing makeup, except for lipstick, which matched the color of the shirt perfectly. Her smile seemed tentative.

"Come in, Deputy Block. Would you like a cup of coffee?"

"Please," he said, adding, "may I have a little sugar in it?"

"Of course." She poured water into the reservoir of a single-cup machine and inserted a pod, lowering the lever toward the mug she had placed to receive the steaming brew. She added a heaping teaspoon of sugar and placed the drink in front of Tony. Then she sat opposite him.

"I'm sorry to report we still don't know who killed your former husband, Ms. Johnson. I wonder if you've had any ideas since you and I met back in October."

"I've thought about it, I really have. I'd like to see whoever killed Brad brought to justice. What he did was a terrible thing, a series of terrible things, but he did his time."

"Let's go back to the trial. You attended every day, is that correct?"

"Every single day, for three weeks, and it was painful—listening to the district attorney laying out the case, listening to all those people talk about how my husband had ruined their lives. As you pointed out, Brad's clients were nice people." She rubbed her temples, as if trying to erase the memory.

"What if one of them wasn't such a nice person? I mean—and I don't really know where I'm going with this—but what if one of them was involved in something nefarious." Tony was impressed with his vocabulary. "What if your husband somehow found out about it…"

"I don't know. If that was the case Brad never said anything to me," Margie said.

"All of his victims, at least those named in the indictment, were Nevadans. His business was based in Las Vegas, and it seems to have been focused around here. But your husband was also licensed in the surrounding states—Utah, Arizona, California, so assumedly he had clients in those states as well. We still don't know what he was doing down in our area. Did he ever travel to Phoenix?"

"I was very involved in my volunteer work here, Deputy Block, and with our kids and their activities—sports, scouts, you know.

Brad took day trips, business trips. I didn't always know where he was going. I'm not sure he even told me. I did fly to Scottsdale with him one time for a meeting—a medical convention of some sort, at the Fairmont Princess hotel. We took a private jet."

Tony tried not to appear over-interested in this information. He waited. Margie seemed to be retrieving the memory from an archived file, then continued.

"They had activities for the wives, spouses I should say—there were a couple of husbands in the group. A trip to the Botanical Gardens, and a cooking demonstration. It was fun. There was a cocktail reception, and a dinner."

"Did you know why, specifically, you and your husband were invited to attend a meeting with a bunch of doctors?"

"Not exactly, but Brad did that kind of thing on occasion, attended professional gatherings. Sometimes he'd sponsor a speaker, or he'd host the coffee break. It was a way to get his name out there, to market his services, to meet new prospects."

"I see. And did he do either of those things at this meeting— sponsor a speaker, I mean, or host a coffee break?"

"I don't think so. But they had an exhibition hall, where vendors who offered services to the medical community had tables set up, with information and swag, you know. Brad had pens with his name on them—they were nice pens—and infor- mation about some of the financial products he sold, and a big bowl of candy. I stopped by to see him between the gardens trip and the cooking."

"I know it's been years, Ms. Johnson, but can you help me narrow the dates for when this meeting took place?" It was prob- ably nothing, but it beat anything else he had to go on.

"As you say, it's been years, decades, actually. But I remember the prickly pears being in full bloom—I never realized they came in so many colors. I'm not a gardener," she added, apologetically.

"So, maybe spring?" He certainly wasn't a gardener either.

"Maybe," she said.

Tony had finished his coffee, and his mind wandered to Maria. Was she sitting outside by the pool? The weather was unseasonably warm for January. They had stored their bags with the valet desk at the Venetian until their rooms were ready, at which time they were told they'd receive a text. They could walk to the concert after dinner. Maria had been in awe of the Strip. He couldn't wait for her to see it at night.

"Thank you again for your time, Ms. Johnson. Please call me if you think of anything, no matter how trivial, that might be helpful to us in finding Brad's killer."

Seventy-four

BY the time he got back to the hotel, their rooms were ready and their bags had been delivered. Maria had texted she was at the pool. He walked down the palatial steps in his street clothes, and spotted her in her swimsuit, reading, in a lounge chair.

Beautiful, inside and out.

She looked up, smiling and waving to him as he approached, indicating the chair next to her.

"Any luck?" she asked, when he sat.

"Maybe," he said. "We'll see."

"Good." She patted his hand. "I'm getting a little hungry. I know you told me to go ahead, but I wanted to wait for you. I've seen some burgers pass by that tempted my palate, but I don't think I can eat a whole one."

"How about we split a burger then, but I want my own beer." He'd introduce her to espresso martinis later. "You order the food, and whatever you'd like to drink, while I go up and change. Get me a local brew—whatever they recommend."

Maria gave him a smile that made him want to invite her right up to his room. He tamped down the thought. *If I'm lucky enough to win this woman's heart, there's a chaste Catholic wedding in my future.* He was willing to wait, to convert, even. *Please, Lord Jesus.*

Maria was worth it.

PART THREE

Seventy-five

JUNE pulled into the driveway at Ray's house. She knew he would have a drink waiting for her, and today, she needed it. It had been hard to leave Jae's side, but she knew from experience the woman would still be alive when she returned to the clinic in the morning. Or, at least, she had felt confident about that an hour ago. It was difficult seeing her friend fail so quickly. She wished Maria were there with her, but she was thrilled her best friend had a man in her life. She had encouraged her to go to Las Vegas with Tony. After all, Maria had worked both Christmas and New Year's Day.

She walked through the front door and Ray greeted her affectionately, taking her jacket and her purse and leading her to the sofa.

"Two martinis coming up," he said.

She smiled, relaxing, once again feeling she was wrong to question their relationship. After all, that whole experience in

Mexico had probably been stressful for Ray, meeting her daughter for the first time. She looked at the ring on her finger. Not everything needed to be articulated; some things could be assumed. That said, she had no intention of giving up her apartment and planned to tell Ray so tonight. She accepted the drink he handed her and tilted her head to receive his kiss.

"How was your day, darling?" she asked. She really had no idea what Ray did during the hours they were apart, except that he seemed to have business interests to attend to, which he did in an office down the hall, the door to which always remained closed. Based on her pleasant surroundings, whatever it was he did, he was successful at it.

"My day was just fine, and now that you're home, it's even better." He squeezed her shoulder, then got up to poke the logs in the fireplace, sending sparks flying up the chimney. June loved a real fire. This really was a beautiful room, and—as large and open as it was—it conveyed a sense of coziness on a cold January night.

"You know, Ray, I really do think of your place as home. It's so warm and inviting, and I love coming here at the end of my shift. I don't know what it is about keeping my own apartment. Maybe it's a sign of my independence, maybe it's the convenience. It's so close to the clinic, and sometimes things come up there at the last minute. I'm touched that you want me here with you all the time, but I really do want to keep my place." There, she'd said it. She congratulated herself on her speech, which she had practiced all day in her head. Maria would be proud.

Ray leaned over and kissed her, taking her empty glass. June allowed him to position her on the sofa, and then to remove her clothes and make love to her. She fell asleep afterward, and when she awoke, covered with the alpaca throw that had been draped over the arm of a chair, she felt momentarily disoriented. She heard cooking sounds, and raised herself on her elbows enough to see Ray at the other end of the long, open room, standing at the stove, stirring what smelled like onions and garlic in a shallow pan. The fragrance was divine. June relaxed, lowering herself back to a reclining position. She still had over forty-eight hours to deal with the matter of the apartment…

Seventy-six

"THE concert was amazing," said Maria, "thank you so much." She touched Tony's arm, and he felt it in his groin. "And you were right about the Vegas lights, and the digital billboards. I've seen pictures, but they don't capture the experience."

They sat on the tarmac at Harry Reid International Airport, waiting to take off on their flight back to Phoenix. It was not quite seven o'clock in the morning. Last night had been more perfect than Tony had anticipated. A romantic dinner at Bouchon at The Venetian, and then a walk across the bridge to the spectacular Sphere. Usually, he was on high alert in a crowd situation—training plus experience—and last night was no exception. But this crowd had been friendly and upbeat, and he found himself letting his guard down, at least a little. The couple sitting next to them had seen the Eagles perform in concert five times, and according to them it never got old. He believed it.

But today, he needed to get home and pursue the meager lead he had into who Brad Hamilton may have known in Arizona. The internet research he'd conducted last night, after walking Maria to her room, indicated that prickly pears begin blooming in the Salt River Valley toward the end of April and were most fully in bloom mid-May. He had called ahead for a subpoena to access guest records at the Fairmont for the months of May in the years 2000 through 2002. Margie thought the convention she remembered attending with her deceased former husband happened pretty close to the time he began fielding accusations of fraudulent behavior by some of his clients. Tony planned to find out when the Hamiltons were at the hotel, then see who else was there at the same time, hoping for an ah-ha moment, maybe a name he had seen previously in the trial transcript.

When they parted at Sky Harbor, Tony kissed Maria and invited her to dinner that night, to which she agreed. He retrieved his car from the onsite parking lot and put the directions to the Fairmont into his navigation system. Thirty minutes later he was standing in the hotel's elegant lobby, looking for signage indicating guest services, where the manager he spoke with while *en route* had agreed to meet him. The necessary paperwork had been delivered, and after showing his credentials Tony and the manager, Michael—a nattily dressed man about his own age—made their way down a hallway past a series of small offices to a room with a desktop computer set up on a table. Two chairs sat before it.

"I've pulled up the logs you requested," said Michael, taking a seat and indicating Tony should do the same. "You're free to scroll through them, taking as much time as you need. We can also do a specific search by name if you like."

"Let's start there," said Tony. "The name is Hamilton. Bradley. Also, when we find the dates he stayed, I'd like the names of any organizations that were having conventions here at the same time."

"That'll be group sales, a different database." The manager typed *Hamilton* into the search bar. *No results*, Tony read from where he sat. He asked Michael to look at 1998, 1999, and 2003. Same.

"Shit," he murmured, under his breath. "She said the prickly pears were in full bloom. That happens in May."

"I beg your pardon?"

"Sorry. Hamilton's wife—former wife—said that when they stayed here, she went on a tour of the botanical gardens, and that the prickly pears were blooming. According to my internet research, that happens in May. That's why I chose that timeframe."

"I see. Yes, our guests often go on group tours—Taliesin West, Musical Instrument Museum, the Heard. Phoenix Botanical Gardens is a favorite. Maybe global warming has affected when the cactus blooms? It surely has affected a lot of other things."

Tony looked at the manager with a whole new respect. "Michael, you're brilliant."

The man beamed.

"I'll get the name of your contact at the gardens. But for the moment, let's assume that, if the temperature's rising, the desert plants may be blooming earlier than they used to. So, maybe twenty years ago, they were in full bloom in June, not May." He shook his head. "Do companies really schedule conferences here in the summer?" Even twenty years ago, he assumed, Phoenix was pretty toasty by June.

"Depends, not if they're coming from Chicago. But local groups…they take advantage of the reduced rates. Those start after Memorial Day."

"Got it. Could you pull up guest registrations for the month of June for those six years? I realize it's not specifically covered in the paperwork."

"It's no problem, Deputy Block. It's within my discretion." He entered the search data, and both men whooped. Mr. and Mrs. Bradley Hamilton had checked into the hotel on Thursday the first, and out on Saturday the third, in June of 2000. The manager minimized the screen and opened a new one, entering search data for conferences being held there during that time frame. Only one, the Healthcare Financial Management Association, appeared.

Tony googled the group on his phone and was impressed by the amount of information that appeared. "These guys are huge," he said. "How many attendees can you handle at one of these events?"

"The Scottsdale Princess has the largest meeting capacity in the Fairmont portfolio," Michael said. His pride in this fact was apparent. "Almost three thousand folks in the ballroom."

"Wow," said Tony. "So this was a big deal. Not sure what Hamilton's interest was—his wife indicated he was marketing his services and had a booth in the exhibition hall. Any idea how I might go about confirming that?"

"You're in luck. The hotel digitized all those files a few years back. Let me see what I can find." Michael typed for a minute, then pointed to a diagram on the screen. "Here's the room set-up for that meeting. Attendees would have used this chart to find the exhibitors they were interested in visiting. I can't vouch for the accuracy—sometimes things get rearranged at the last minute. You know, someone didn't need an electrical outlet and now they do, that kind of thing. This is the key, telling you who had which booth." He indicated a series of numbers, with names beside them.

Tony squinted at the small print, praying he'd find the name Hamilton. Michael maximized the screen, then pointed with his finger to a square in the corner of the room. "It looks like your man was located next to the coffee service—that's prime real estate."

"Can you tell who's on his other side?" asked Tony.

"Looks like a company called Med-Cap. I can dig a little deeper if you like, probably come up with a personal contact. Would you like me to print this off for you?"

"That'd be great, thank you."

"Happy to help," said Michael. "Your requests are timely. We just contracted with a national IT company that'll be getting rid of old files we no longer need. If you had come around a week from now, this information would have disappeared into the ether."

Seventy-seven

TONY rose to introduce himself and shake hands with the elderly man who walked his way. His gait was spry, no shuffling.

"Nice to meet you, Deputy Block. Please sit down. You know, I can go months without a visitor, but yours is the second I've had in as many days."

"Oh, really?" said Tony, politely.

"Yes, a mystery writer, wanted to know more about my business."

"And what business is that, Mr. McBride?"

"Charlie, call me Charlie, makes me feel younger. My business was medical billing, company was Med-Cap. Sold it in 2002. No longer exists, I'm sorry to say."

"I see. Do you remember attending a conference in Scottsdale back in June of 2000, the Healthcare Financial Management Association?"

"Sure. That's a big one, the gold standard. Those people wrote the book on hospital revenue cycles—those are fancy words for billing. They've been around since the fifties, forties maybe, developed certification programs, elevated hospital financial management to a profession. Their work got more challenging every year, what with the expansion of Medicare and all. What's your interest?"

"Actually, my interest is in another attendee at that conference, a man by the name of Bradley Hamilton."

"Well, why didn't you say so? Brad was there at my request. His firm handled all of Med-Cap's benefits—health insurance, life insurance, retirement plans, the works. Helped me with my personal planning, too. Great guy—smart guy. I understand he got into some trouble later on, after I sold the business. Too bad. Working around money can sometimes be too much temptation, I guess. Especially other people's money."

"Are you aware of what's happened to Brad?" asked Tony.

"Last I heard he got out of prison for good behavior. But twenty years behind bars would be hard to come back from."

"I hate to be the bearer of bad news, Mr. McBride, Charlie, I mean, but Brad Hamilton was murdered over in Cave Creek almost three months ago. We're trying to find out who did it. It seems many people have cause, but so far, we haven't come up with a suspect."

"Oh, no, I'm sorry to hear that, Deputy Block. As I said, Brad Hamilton was a trusted advisor to our company."

"Any idea who might have wanted to see him dead?"

"I can't imagine such a thing."

"I appreciate your time, Mr. McBride. Here's my card, in case you think of anything. By the way, who took over the company after you sold it?"

"A key employee bought it from me, my chief financial officer. Ray Prentiss, P-R-E-N-T-I-S-S."

Seventy-eight

TONY started his engine to get the air moving, then checked his phone for messages. A text from Maria brought him down.

Something came up at work that may keep me from going out tonight. An emoji with a teardrop was only a small consolation.

Tony had been planning the evening as he investigated the Hamilton case. He was going to tell Maria about the call he received from his stepsister on Christmas day, and about subsequent emails they had exchanged. These communications had brought closure to the conflict he felt with respect to Lizzy, and had given him an emotional green light to pursue Maria with his whole heart. The fact was, he was crazy about her. He had even envisioned a scene in which he visited her brother, Frank, and their mother, Aurelia, to ask for Maria's hand in marriage. Some might think it was too soon, but he just *knew.* He was so certain that he'd thought about buying a ring, but he didn't have quite that level of confidence yet.

Oh, well, for now he needed to put these thoughts aside and find this Ray Prentiss fellow. According to McBride, his protégé turned successor would surely have continued working with Brad Hamilton. It was a long shot, but perhaps Prentiss could provide some piece of information that would be useful in solving the murder at Rancho Manana.

Seventy-nine

TONY rang the doorbell, then used the knocker on the heavy, carved wooden door. According to a quick internet search, Ray Prentiss had lived at the secluded home on the large lot in Scottsdale for the past twenty years. Thank goodness for GPS. The house number was almost impossible to read from the street.

Tony had started to call—he typically made an appointment for this type of interview. But today, he had decided to forge ahead, hoping to get the conversation out of the way, praying that he and Maria might still be getting together tonight.

A man Tony placed in his mid-to-late fifties, maybe early sixties, answered the door. Tall, clean cut, well dressed in a casual, *GQ* style. In the background Tony heard a woman's voice. "Ray, have you seen my purse? I can't find it."

Good. He had the right house.

"Yes?"

"Ray Prentiss?"

"Yes?"

"Are you the Ray Prentiss who once owned Med-Cap?"

"Yes, that's me. What's this about?"

"I'm Tony Block, sheriff's deputy with Maricopa County, District Four." As he introduced himself, he held out his identification. "You're not in any kind of trouble, but I'd like to ask you a few questions about someone you may have known years ago. May I come in?"

"Of course, officer. This is my wife, June. Please have a seat, Deputy Block. Can I get you anything?"

"A glass of water would be nice, thank you."

From the kitchen at the end of the long, cavernous room, Tony heard Prentiss's wife ask again if he had seen her purse. She spoke quietly, but he made out the words 'phone' and 'keys'. Prentiss assured her he would help her look as soon as he finished talking with the officer. He spoke patiently, as if to a child. Another reason to make this conversation brief, thought Tony.

Eighty

"SMITH here, how can I help you?" Trevor sat in his office at District Four headquarters, speaking into his desk phone. The receptionist had buzzed him, asking if he was available to talk. The caller had initially asked for Tony Block.

"Deputy Smith, my name is Tim Koenig. I'm a parole officer with the Nevada Department of Corrections."

"What can I do for you, Mr. Koenig?"

"Several months ago, one of your men, Deputy Block, visited me here in connection with the murder of one of my parolees, Bradley Hamilton."

Trevor leaned forward in his chair. "Yes?"

"He told me to call if anything came up that might be helpful in your investigation. Well, something did come up, although I have no idea whether it will be helpful or not."

"Go on," Trevor encouraged. Anything would be helpful at this point.

"I'm working with a recently released man who was in minimum security with Hamilton, there toward the end. Man's name is Lewenski, Mordecai Lewenski. He worked in corporate finance, got caught embezzling from his employer. Said it was just too easy, and he needed the money. Anyway, he and Hamilton apparently hit it off, probably because they were both intelligent, white-collar criminals, not like most of these guys. Brad shared something with Mordy that may not mean a thing. But, like I said, Deputy Block asked me to call…"

"You ever worked a jigsaw puzzle, Koenig?"

"Huh? I mean, sure. Does that have something to do with the murder?"

"As you know, Koenig, sometimes you get to a point where you're sure you've lost one of the pieces. You pat around on the carpet under the table for it, then you wonder if a mistake was made at the factory, then you become convinced the dog chewed it up. But if you just keep plodding along, eventually that piece, which was there all along, shows up, and then everything else falls into place." Trevor leaned back in his chair, never more satisfied with himself than when he waxed philosophical.

The line was quiet. Was Koenig scratching his head?

"I think I get your point, Deputy Smith. Any one clue might be that missing piece that moves the investigation toward solution. Well, here goes. Apparently, Hamilton told Lewinski he had been working with a company that was very successful, and a good client, no mention of a name. In the course of their dealings, Hamilton placed a big investment, only to discover it was being funded with stolen money. But he needed the commission—he was in pretty deep by then—so he didn't report it. And, after all, that would be kind of hypocritical, although it seems Hamilton never thought of himself as a thief.

"Hamilton told Lewinski that if he ever managed to get out, he planned to seek employment with that company. He assumed, knowing what he knew, and them knowing that he knew, they'd agree to pay him a hefty salary."

"Blackmail," said Trevor.

"One could call it that. As I'm sure you know, it's not easy for the men we try to help to find jobs, and certainly not the kind of work that pays what Hamilton, or Lewinski, for that matter, had been making."

"This may be helpful, Koenig, thanks for the call. I'll pass it along to Block. He's taken the lead on this one, and may be back in touch."

"You're welcome. As I stated back in October, Brad Hamilton was an agreeable sort. He paid his dues, and I thought he had a future. I'd like to see his killer found. Good luck, Deputy Smith."

Eighty-one

JUNE exited the kitchen through the double sliding doors and sat down in a recliner by the pool. Her mind flashed back to the first time she had been on this patio. That day last October had been hot, and the pool, and the chilled martini, cool and refreshing. She shivered.

Today was cold and dreary, and Ray had convinced her to call in sick, even though she had told him, in no uncertain terms, that she didn't want to. She hated lying, and lately it seemed she did it a lot—to Savannah, to Maria, to herself. She decided to take a short nap. She hadn't slept well, and she felt tired and discouraged. She hadn't figured out yet what to do about the movers. And now she couldn't find her purse.

She went through the sliding door that led to her bedroom, intending to do another search there. Nothing. She walked out into the hall that led to Ray's bedroom, to his office, and back toward the great room. The door to the large, open living area stood ajar; she could hear the men talking. The door at the other end of the hall was closed, as always. She had never been in it, hadn't had a reason to be. There was next to no chance her personal belongings could be there.

She opened the door a crack. The room was dimly lit by a window with southwestern exposure, its shades pulled almost closed, but not entirely, so that the sun created shadows, like slats, on the opposite wall. She made out a desk, with neat stacks of papers and mail. There was a bookshelf; she couldn't make out any titles.

She jumped when she heard the front door close, pulled the office door quietly shut, and ducked into her room. Lying on the bed, she pretended to sleep, although still wearing her shoes, as Ray walked past.

Eighty-two

TONY pulled away from the house and took a quick driving tour of the surrounding Arcadia neighborhood. Stately homes on large lots, meticulous landscapes with mature trees, an occasional Mercedes or Bentley turning into a long receding driveway. Old money. Or new money with class. Whatever. He was certainly no sociologist, although he had taken a course in college.

He turned onto Camelback Road with the intention of heading to the station in Carefree before going home to retrieve Rusty from the neighbor who was dog sitting. But with rush hour traffic, he realized it would be over an hour before he got there. And, it had started to rain, adding to the dreariness of the day. He pulled into a strip mall parking lot and saw that he had missed a call from his superior. His return call went to voicemail.

"Sorry I missed your call. I'm in south Scottsdale, just followed up on a dead-end lead. Talk to you later." He set the phone into its mounted holder and pulled back out onto the road. He wondered if he should call Maria, but he was sure she knew how much he wanted to see her, and he assumed she would let him know if she could make their date. He hoped her work situation had resolved itself. Providentially, the phone rang, and her name appeared on the screen.

"Hello?" he said, eagerly.

"Hi, Tony, how's your day going?"

"Better, now that I'm talking to you. Any chance we can get together?"

"I think I can do that, around seven o'clock. I'll come to your place, with Chinese, does that sound good? I need to get back to the clinic first thing tomorrow, so I can't stay long. We're short-staffed."

"That sounds great, thank you!"

Tony's spirit soared, and he again had the thought of stopping into a jewelry store to look at engagement rings. He had a little time to kill. Coming up, on his right, was a modest store with a huge sign—The Diamond Guys—above the door. No kidding? He turned in and parked. This is practice, he thought, taking a deep breath and exiting the car, reaching back for his phone. It vibrated. Trevor.

"Hey man, what's up?"

"You got a minute?"

"Sure, nothing happening here." He got back into the car. *Whew, dodged a bullet.*

"That guy Koenig you interviewed up in Reno called— you know, Hamilton's parole officer. Since you weren't here, I talked to him."

"Yeah, I remember him."

"Another inmate shared some information, got out a couple of weeks early for it. Hamilton told him he intended to ask a former client in Phoenix for a job—said the client had a reason to do him a favor. That could be why he was down here."

"Got it. Makes sense that he had multiple clients down here. We just need to discover who they were. I talked to an older gentleman earlier, spoke highly of Brad, said he was a trusted advisor to his business. Then I interviewed the guy who bought the company from him, but he replaced Brad—said something didn't seem quite right about him. Probably saved him from getting caught in Hamilton's web."

"Two down, who knows how many to go."

"I'm on it; talk to you later."

Eighty-three

TONY was waiting for Maria's knock when it came. He had gotten out placemats, utensils, and napkins, and chilled a bottle of white wine he had stopped for on his way home. Rusty had recovered from the excitement of reuniting with his master and now lay quietly in his bed in the corner, head resting on his front paws, watching Tony's every move. At her knock, he barked sharply and jumped out of the bed, stretching his body from the tips of his front paws to his tail, preparing to greet the woman Tony had confided to him gave him almost as much joy as Rusty did.

Maria laughed and handed Tony a white paper bag, kneeling to take Rusty's face in her hands, ruffling his muzzle and scratching the fur behind his ears. Tony smiled and set the bag down, taking in the warmth of this woman he was falling head over heels in love with. Feeling suddenly shy, he kissed her cheek, helped to remove her rain jacket, and guided her by the elbow to the sofa, handing her one of two glasses of wine he brought from the kitchen.

"So, tell me about your day," he said, settling himself beside her as Rusty licked her ankles and she giggled.

"It was fine," she said. "As I've told you, we have a lovely patient who's in her final hours after a short but valiant battle with breast cancer. Her nurse, my friend, June, called in sick today, which is bad timing. But really, at this point, we're just administering morphine and making her comfortable. It's hard to know how aware people are, you know, when they're passing over. We soothe them and keep their lips moist, and shift them periodically, to prevent bed sores. Sorry, this isn't great cocktail conversation, is it?" Maria smiled, sadly.

Tony knew his own mother had gone through a similar illness when he was a child, too young to really understand what was happening, and he hoped the nurse who had cared for her had been as pretty and compassionate as Maria.

"It's fine," he said. "I'm sorry things are hard right now. Ironically, the guy I interviewed this afternoon was married to a woman named June. You don't hear that name around here very often."

"No," said Maria. "My friend is from North Carolina—very beautiful, and very sweet. She speaks with a southern drawl."

"I don't know about this woman," said Tony. "She was attractive, but she didn't say much, and she didn't hang around. Hungry?"

"Sure am, the food smells yummy. I had to keep myself from eating one of the wontons while I was driving. Now that I think of it, I'm pretty sure I skipped lunch today."

Eighty-four

JUNE waited until she was sure Ray was in the shower, then quickly crept back into his office. She had decided during dinner to wait for an opportunity to search the room. Ray acted unconcerned about the personal items she had 'misplaced'—that was the word he used—while she struggled to hold her anxiety at bay. Now, she opened the door to the room at the end of the hall, and turned on the ceiling fixture, a combination light and fan, ears attentive to the sound of running water coming from the primary bath.

The room looked different under the artificial glare. She surveyed it quickly, then moved toward the desk. She shuffled through the unopened envelopes stacked neatly on its surface. Statements from multiple banks, brokerage houses, and insurance companies—tax reporting documents, apparently—it was that time of year. She opened a file drawer that looked big enough to hold her bag, and froze. A handgun.

No need to panic, Junie. A lot of men own guns, don't they? Greg had one. That was among the reasons she'd left him. Guns and anger management issues didn't mix well, especially with a child in the house. She shuddered as she remembered the fear she had felt for herself, and for Savannah. The water stopped running. She had seconds before Ray would emerge from the shower and take his towel from the hook on the wall, perhaps wrapping it around his body and calling to her. She closed the drawer quietly and slipped from the room.

Eighty-five

"TONY, I need to go now. Thank you again for the fun get-away. I have a totally different perspective on Las Vegas than I did before. I'm not sure what tomorrow looks like for me, but I'll check in with you when I can. I'm nervous June will call in sick again, and I'm worried about her. Her boyfriend told her—told her, mind you—that she was moving out of her apartment and into his house."

"What?"

"You heard me right. I hope she's digging in her heels. I've never met the guy, although I've tried. He sounds like the kind of control freak we talked about in our group. I'm concerned June has gotten herself into a relationship she can't get out of. Her daughter's concerned, too. She called me on Christmas Eve from Mexico. It wasn't really the clinic I took that call from."

The intensity in Maria's voice communicated her frustration. Tony could tell she was distressed, and wished he knew something helpful to say. Instead, he responded lamely, "It must be hard, seeing your friend in this situation. Please let me know if I can do anything."

"Thank you. I wish I could think of something. What does your day look like tomorrow?" Maria asked as she rose to go. Tony stood, too.

"I need to return to this senior living place and talk to this older gentleman again. He used to be a client of Brad Hamilton, the guy who was killed. We got a tip today. Hamilton may have been coming to the area to try to get a job with a former client. I need to find out what other clients he had here. Hopefully McBride can provide some additional intel. Fingers crossed."

"Good luck." She gave him an encouraging smile, then wrapped her arms around his waist and presented her lips for him to kiss. Tony's courage soared. He promised himself a visit to the first jewelry store he passed tomorrow, after meeting with McBride.

Eighty-six

"**Deputy** Block, welcome back. Would you like a cup of coffee?" Charles McBride indicated a self-service station in a corner of the well-appointed room, complete with pottery mugs featuring the center's logo. Most important—for Tony—was the basket filled with paper packets of sugar. He brewed himself a cup and stirred in two of them, then sat across from McBride. It was then that he noticed the book the old gentleman was reading, and recognized the title.

"You like mysteries?" he asked.

"I like most genres," McBride replied. "When you get to be my age, you have plenty of time on your hands. Reading helps to fill it. But this particular novel," he said, pausing to hold it up for Tony to get a better look, "was written by that lady that came to visit me a few days ago. I happened to see it in our library here after she left, so I borrowed it. It's good. Well written. Believable characters. I haven't finished it yet, so I can't tell you whether it has a satisfying ending or not. What brings you back?"

"A couple of things, actually. We're thinking now that Brad Hamilton may have been in the Phoenix area to apply for a job, perhaps with a former client of his. You said you liked working with him, considered him a valuable advisor. We're looking for other business owners like yourself who may have felt the same way. Does anyone fitting that description come to mind?"

McBride seemed to be thinking, then shook his head. "You know, it's been over twenty years…"

"I understand," Tony said, "I was just hoping… Do you happen to remember the name of the insurance company, or companies, whose products Hamilton sold you?"

Again, McBride seemed to be searching for information long filed away in his brain. "Security? I think that may have been part of it. Did you talk to Prentiss? Maybe he remembers."

Tony was reluctant to tell Charles McBride that his successor hadn't trusted the financial advisor he had chosen. "I'll ask him," he said. Then, "By the way, just out of curiosity, what were the terms of the sale—of your business, I mean." It was obvious McBride was living a comfortable life here in the Vi at Grayhawk community.

"We structured a buy-out," McBride said, "based on a formula that included the company's book value and a percentage of its current and future earnings. As I may have mentioned to you, those were both down at the time, due to the overall economy. The buyout was to take place over a ten-year period, but Ray paid me off after the first twelve months. That wasn't so great, for multiple reasons, including my tax bill. In hindsight, I should have thought about inserting a pre-payment clause."

Tony's law enforcement training didn't include much business education—just an introductory accounting course—and he was feeling out of his element. Nor could he see the relevance of this information in solving the murder of Brad Hamilton. He thanked Charles McBride for meeting with him again, and stood to shake hands and go.

"If you happen to run into Ms. Scott," said McBride, "tell her I like the book, and that I'm looking forward to reading the next one when it's available."

"If I run into her," said Tony, "I'll tell her."

"Oh, and that insurance company Hamilton worked with…"

"Yes?"

"It was based in Denver."

Eighty-seven

JUNE pulled away as Ray attempted to grope her from behind. "I don't have time for that right now, Ray, I need to get to the clinic. My patient is dying. Either take me there or call me an Uber."

"And who *is* your patient, June? Are you going to let me in on your little secret when she's gone?"

"For God's sake, Ray, it'll be all over the news when she's gone! Is that what this is about?"

"I'm just saying, if you really loved me, you wouldn't keep secrets from me."

"And I'm saying, if *you* really loved *me*, you'd stop trying to control me. But if you must know, God damn it, Jacque Mace is at the Mayo, and she's dying, and I need to be with her. And you're accusing *me* of keeping secrets? Where the hell is my purse? I've torn this place apart looking for it. Things don't just disappear into thin air—you're hiding it from me. But why? So you can keep me a prisoner in your house? And what kind of business are you in, anyway?"

"Jacque Mace? *The* Jacque Mace?"

"Yes, Ray, the one and only. Now would you please take me to the clinic? We can look for my keys later. I didn't mean the things I said, I'm just upset, and tired. I didn't sleep well."

"It's okay, baby. I understand. Let's go. I'll take you. And I'll pick you up later when you get off."

Eighty-eight

TONY was driving toward Carefree, scanning the street on both sides for possibilities, when he saw the Shane Co. sign. Immediately, the company's famous ad popped into his head, "now *you* have a friend in the diamond business". *We'll just see about that.* He pulled into the parking lot, checked his phone for messages, and took out his pocket comb to straighten his hair before exiting his Maricopa County patrol car and walking into the store. A woman about his age walked toward him, smiling.

"Good morning. May I help you?"

"I'm not sure," Tony said, "I think I'd like to look at engagement rings."

The woman smiled her encouragement. "Of course," she said. "We have many beautiful rings to choose from. Let's try to narrow it down. Is there a price range you would like to stay within?"

Oh, shit. He hadn't really gotten that far in his thinking. "Um, well, I'm kind of on a budget, and I guess I don't really know how much things like this cost." She could see he was a cop, right? And most people knew cops were underpaid, right? Especially when you considered the risks.

"We have rings in all price ranges, from fifty dollars to well over five thousand. Tell me about your fiancée."

"Well, her name is Maria. She's a nurse. She's very pretty, and she has a very nice family. But I haven't asked her to marry me yet."

"I understand. I'll bet she's going to say 'yes' when you do. But if for some reason that isn't the case, you may return any of our rings for a full refund. Let's look at some of your options. I'm guessing a woman who works in Maria's profession and has to wash her hands often during the day might like something simple. Simple, but elegant."

Tony nodded, grateful for the feminine guidance. Twenty minutes later, he handed over his credit card for the purchase of a classic, four-prong solitaire engagement ring in fourteen karat yellow gold. When he walked out of the store, he felt a hundred feet tall. He'd get to headquarters, research Denver insurance companies, and then try to meet with Frank Chavez to ask for Maria's hand in marriage.

Eighty-nine

FRANK greeted Tony with a handshake and led him down the hall to his office. He kept his door open, except when he sensed a person's need for confidentiality. He closed it now, and motioned Tony to a round table with four chairs in a corner of the room.

"It's good to see you, Tony. What brings you over to Fountain Hills?"

"It's about Maria…"

"Is there a problem?" Frank knew his sister had flown to Las Vegas with Tony, and she seemed to be growing quite fond of him.

"No, no, not at all. It's just that…well…I'm in love with Maria, and I'd like to ask her to marry me."

Frank laughed in relief. "Well then do it, man!" he said.

Tony laughed too—also, it seemed, in relief.

"I thought I should speak with you about it first."

"That's thoughtful of you Tony, but this is 2025, and my sister is a grown woman. She speaks for herself. But when you do ask her, you can tell her that I think you'd make a fine husband, and a good brother-in-law."

"Thank you, sir, Frank, thank you very much."

"You're most welcome. Now, tell me, deputy, how's that case coming over in Cave Creek? Any idea who murdered that guy by the pool?"

"Not yet, but we have a working theory. We think Brad Hamilton—that's the guy's name, you may recall—was in the area to ask a former client of his for a job. He had some compromising information, apparently, that gave him reason to expect to be hired."

"And you think the client knocked him off?"

"Maybe. Anyway, we need to develop a list of his Arizona clients. Hamilton did business with multiple insurance companies, at least one of them located in Denver, but from my basic research so far there are quite a few to choose from—home offices, regional offices, brokerage firms, agencies—those terms run together for me, and I'm not sure where to start. I've got a lot of phone calls to make."

"I know someone who might be able to help you narrow it down," Frank said. John Crouch, whom he had once considered a murder suspect in a case over in Tonto Verde, was a highly successful advisor with McDougal Partners, a firm specializing in wealth management. Frank liked John, and still had his phone number in his contacts, although he hadn't seen him in months. "Want me to give him a call?"

"You bet, why not?"

"Deputy Chavez?" The surprise in John's voice, projecting from the phone's speaker, was unmistakable. Apparently, John Crouch had kept *his* contact information as well.

"That's right, John, it's me, Frank. How've you been since I last saw you at the Harrington House opening?"

"Fine, fine, Frank. Thank you for asking. Business is great, and Jennifer is in her element, busier than ever, and making new friends wherever she goes. Life is good. But obviously, you're calling for a reason. What can I do for you?"

"I'm sitting here with a colleague from over in Carefree, District Four, Deputy Tony Block. He's been investigating a murder that took place in Cave Creek, at the Rancho Manana resort, a guy by the name of Brad Hamilton."

There was a brief silence before John responded, "I know the name."

"You know much about him?" Frank said.

"Only that he was trouble," John said, "and now he's dead. I never met Hamilton personally."

"Do you know anyone who did?" Frank said.

"Rumor is, he approached my partners years ago about offering their proprietary products to his clients. He also asked for concessions, advances against business in underwriting, that kind of thing. I guess some of the insurance companies he worked with were willing. The guy obviously had balls—I'll give him that."

"But they turned him down," Frank said. *My partners.* John really *was* doing well, and Frank was happy for him.

"In no uncertain terms," said John.

Tony leaned in. "John, Tony Block here. Thanks for the information. Regarding the insurance companies Hamilton worked with—do you happen to know any of their names?"

"I don't," John said. "But I'd be happy to ask James and Steve if they remember."

"That could be helpful—thanks!"

"No problem. If you don't mind holding, they're both in the office now, I think. Just give me a minute…"

The two deputies exchanged looks, then Frank took their coffee cups to the kitchenette down the hall for refills, leaving Tony to listen to on-hold music. As Frank returned to his office, John Crouch came back on the line.

"At that point in time," he said, "according to James McDougal, Hamilton was doing a lot of business with a Denver-based company, Secure Alliance. It's a good company, we work with them too. Great client service."

Ninety

TONY Block sat staring at his computer screen. Trevor Smith stopped by and shot him a questioning look. Tony shook his head. "Nothing yet," he said. Then, "Hold on, here it comes."

Trevor pulled up a chair and joined him in front of the screen as he decrypted the attachment he had just received from the vice-president of administration at the Secure Alliance Insurance Company. He had sent the subpoena for a list of Bradley Hamilton's policyholders to the company's legal department, after phoning them with an explanation. That was just an hour ago. John Crouch wasn't kidding—the company's service was amazing. The document was several pages long, and while he waited for the printer to do its job, he scanned the list of names. One jumped out. *Raymond Prentiss.*

"Wait of minute," he said, "this guy said he fired Hamilton."

"Huh?"

"That guy I met over in Scottsdale, the one who bought out the old man who used to own the medical billing enterprise? He told me he didn't trust Hamilton. Said when he bought the company he stopped doing business with him. But here's his name—Raymond L. Prentiss, 2002, Variable Annuity, $5,000,000—holy shit, five million dollars? I think I may have a few more questions for Mr. Prentiss."

Ninety-one

"**FRANK?**"

"Hey, Sis, what's up?" Frank didn't mention to Maria that her boyfriend had left his office not two hours ago, with a ring intended for her in the pocket of his uniform.

"It's June. We have to help her. She's at work now, and we can't let her go back to Ray's. He has a gun in the house. But her car's there, and her keys and her phone. We have to get her out of there and find a safe place for her to stay. She agrees. But it's complicated. And for now, we're both tied to the clinic, waiting for Jane Doe to pass."

"I'll see what I can do," Frank said, although he had no idea what he would, or should, or even could do, unless June filed a complaint.

"Nancy, I need your help again. Please call me back. Thanks in advance." Frank felt compelled to make his way over to Prentiss's house, not knowing what would happen when he got there. Whatever it was, he didn't want to arrive in his official, black SUV with *Sheriff* emblazoned in foot-high gold lettering on the sides. His author friend returned his call immediately.

"Sorry I missed you, Frank, I was shlepping groceries!" Nancy sounded breathless, as usual.

"No worries, and I hate to trouble you, especially if you just got home from shopping in Fountain Hills. But I was wondering if you might take a field trip with me, and if you'd be willing to drive. I'll pay for the gas."

"Sure thing! Sounds intriguing. Let me put things in the fridge and I'll be right there!"

The golf community of Tonto Verde, and the town of Fountain Hills, were only ten miles apart. But it took twice as many minutes to drive the distance between them, due to the forty-five miles-per-hour speed limit posted in McDowell Mountain Regional Park, which separated the two. When Nancy pulled up in front of the town hall, where the District Seven sheriff's office was located, Frank was waiting.

"Hop in!" she said, "and tell me where we're going."

"Please drive me to the house Ray Prentiss lives in," he said. He described the brief phone conversation with Maria while Nancy pulled up the phone contact and activated her navigation app. "I'm not sure what I'm going to do when I get there, without a restraining order, or a search warrant, or anything else official."

Thirty-five minutes later they drove slowly past the secluded home. A Maricopa County sheriff's vehicle was parked in the driveway behind a car Frank recognized as June's. "What the f-heck? Keep driving, Nancy. Pull around the corner, please."

He texted his sister: *Is June there with you?*

Yes why? she replied instantly.

Just confirming.

"Let's drive by again," he said, struggling to make sense of the situation. This time, when they passed the house, Frank recognized Tony and watched him get into his car.

"Wait for him to pull out, then follow him," he instructed Nancy. When they had driven a short distance from the house and were stopped at a cross-street, she pulled alongside as Frank lowered his window and got Tony's attention.

"What's going on?" Tony said.

"That's what I'd like to know," Frank said. "Let's stop at the first coffee shop we see and huddle." He and Nancy let Tony take the lead. He turned right onto Scottsdale Boulevard, and almost immediately into the parking lot of an old mom and pop place in need of a paint job. The three seated themselves at a corner table and ordered three black coffees—one with sugar—and a half dozen assorted donuts.

Frank introduced Nancy to Tony, who chuckled.

"Mr. Charles McBride asked me, if I saw you, to tell you he liked your book. I said I would, but of course, I wasn't really expecting to see you…" He shook his head in confusion.

"I'll go first," Frank said. "I asked Nancy to drive me over. She has great intuition—one of the qualities that makes her such a good mystery writer, no doubt—and, I wanted to be anonymous. Maria's friend, June, goes with the creep who lives in that house; at least, that's who we think lives in the house, guy by the name of Ray Prentiss?"

"Yes…he lives there…" Tony said, a look of apprehension on his face. "June…that guy's wife is Maria's friend?"

"They're not married," said Frank. "Did he tell you they were? What were you doing there, anyway?"

"I'm trying to find out who Bradley Hamilton drove down from Reno to meet with, someone he'd worked with. Anyway,

Prentiss told me he didn't work with Hamilton after he bought the business from McBride. However, the insurance company says otherwise, to the tune of five million dollars. Thanks again for connecting me to John Crouch. I called him back, and he gave me a crash course on annuities."

Nancy looked up at the mention of her good friend's name, then went back to whatever she was doing on her phone. Frank had never known her to be silent for so long. He asked Tony, "So, what did Prentiss have to say?"

"He wasn't there. Another man answered the door, said he was a houseguest of Prentiss's. The guy had weird hair—braided, with tattoos—but well-dressed. Still, not exactly someone you'd expect to be hanging out with a retired business exec."

"I knew it!" said Nancy. "It was the Biketoberally!"

At this point in their relationship, Frank had far too much respect to discount anything his friend said. But he realized he was looking at her as if she'd lost her mind. Ditto for Tony.

"Please say more, Detective," said Frank, which brought on that amazing smile of hers.

"The day Hamilton was killed was the first day of the Biketoberally—thousands of bikers descending on Cave Creek. Just saying…"

A look of mutual comprehension passed between Frank and Tony. "The distraction…" said Frank.

Ninety-two

JUNE concluded the five-minute observation period during which she confirmed that Jae had stopped breathing and had no pulse. She squeezed her friend's hand and pulled the top bed sheet over her head. She dabbed at her own cheek with a tissue, wiping away tears as she quietly closed the door behind her and returned to her station to call the hospital morgue. Ray had never visited her at the clinic, so June was shocked to see him standing there.

"What…how did you…who let you back here?" she stammered.

"Aren't you happy to see me?" he said. What she had once considered an irresistible smile now seemed menacing. June looked around. Things were unseasonably quiet at the Mayo today, not another person in sight. *Stay calm.*

"Of course," she said. "But I can't visit now, I need to make an important call. And my shift isn't over for another three hours."

"I thought you might be able to get off early, since tomorrow's your moving day." Now he leered at her, and June gripped the edge of her desk. "But I don't mind waiting for you in the reception area. I brought some reading material with me."

Ninety-three

NANCY retrieved a notebook and pencil from her large satchel handbag. "This mystery is ready to be solved," she declared. "Deputy Block, you walk us through it. I'll take notes."

Tony, taken aback by this red-haired dynamo, complied, methodically leading his companions through the interviews he'd held, the facts he'd uncovered, and the suspicions he'd developed, gaining confidence as he went. Although he wasn't sure where he was going when he began, he ended up concluding—as he assumed Nancy and Frank already had—that Ray Prentiss had killed Brad Hamilton by the pool at Rancho Manana, in broad daylight, against the thundering backdrop of a thousand motorcycles rumbling down Cave Creek Road, less than a mile away. Prentiss had embezzled funds from McBride's company, funds he used to purchase a large deferred annuity from Hamilton after buying Med-Cap at a deep discount, using an early distribution from the annuity to pay off the note. Hamilton had figured out that the funds were stolen, but he needed the sales commission, so he said nothing. Prentiss knew that Hamilton knew, and when he got in touch after his release from prison, there was really only one way out of the situation.

"But we lack physical evidence," Tony concluded. "And how does June figure into all of this?"

Frank sighed. "That, my friend," he said, "is just a case of bad luck, which unfortunately the lady attracts. But one thing's for sure, she's about to part ways with her boyfriend. And you and your buddies need to get a warrant and search that house. My hunch is you'll find what you need to justify an arrest."

Ninety-four

MARIA found June in the bathroom. She had obviously been crying and was now attempting to repair her makeup.

"I don't know what to do," June said. "Ray's waiting for me in the reception area. I'm scared."

"Just stay in here for now, June, and lock the door. I need to think." *And to get in touch with my brother.*

Ninety-five

WHEN deputies Tony Block and Trevor Smith arrived at the Mayo Clinic in Scottsdale, they spotted Frank Chavez and Nancy Scott parked in an unobtrusive corner of the lot, under the shade of a huge Blue Palo Verde. They got out and approached the car.

"So, now who's out of their territory?" Frank said, rolling down the window on the passenger side of Nancy's car to tease his old friend, and his soon-to-be brother-in-law. At least that's what he hoped. Trevor laughed.

"You were right," Tony said. "We found a treasure trove of illegal drugs, and a cache of checkbooks from banks all over the state, each opened with an initial cash deposit of ten thousand dollars, according to the registers. An old-fashioned calendar in Prentiss's desk drawer had an entry for a meeting at Rancho Manana back in October, on the day Hamilton died. We found a purse buried under some laundry in Prentiss's closet—driver's license indicates it's June's. We found her passport in another location in the house. And you'll be flattered to know, Nancy, that there was a copy of your book. It's all circumstantial, but we think we'll be able to make the case. We're here to arrest him."

"But what are you two doing here?" Trevor said.

"Just making sure June stays safe. Maria texted to say Prentiss was waiting for her to get off work. She doesn't want to leave with him. Nancy and I thought we'd hang around to make sure she didn't have to. It sounds like you'll be taking care of that problem. How did you know where to find him?"

"That houseguest, Raul?" Tony said. "He told us he met Prentiss at Christmas, at a hotel bar. They exchanged cards. Prentiss got in touch recently and asked him to fly to Phoenix and drive him and his fiancée down to Mexico, said they were looking to move there. The guy is in the business of providing security. He said when June got off work, they planned to pick him up at the house and head out of town.

"We don't have anything on him—yet—but we confiscated his phone and asked him to come to the station while we conducted the search. He's there with Jack now. Well, we'd better go in and get the bastard."

"Quick question," Frank said. "June told Maria that Prentiss hid a gun in a drawer in his office. Did you find it?"

The two men looked at each other and shook their heads. "No gun," Tony said.

Ninety-six

WHAT'S *happening now?* Frank texted Maria.

June's locked in the water closet. Ray's in the lobby. Where are you?

In the parking lot, waiting for reinforcements. We'll be there soon. Stay safe.

Within minutes six of the thirty full-time deputies out of District Seven screeched into the parking lot, lights flashing, no sirens. Frank barked orders as the men and women arrived. "Secure the exits. Guard the windows. Suspect is armed and dangerous. Let's take him alive."

"Stay down," he warned Nancy, whose excitement was palpable, as he and Tony headed toward the hospital entrance, Trevor close on their heels.

Ninety-seven

JUNE sat on the toilet, in the dark, just feet away from the nurses' station, thinking about the patients whose needs she should be attending to, and about the patient who had become her friend and who had just passed. She needed to call Jae's family, as she had promised she would. She needed to call her landlord and beg him not to rent her apartment to anyone else. She needed to find her phone and her keys, and to retrieve her car from Ray's driveway. She gripped the edges of the seat. Her stomach felt like it was tied up in knots. The tension in her body made it difficult to breathe.

Suddenly she heard Ray's voice. "You must be Maria."

"Yes, I am. I'm the head nurse supervisor here. What can I help you with?"

"I'm looking for my fiancée, your friend, June. She should be getting off work about now. We're leaving on a trip, and we need to get home and pack."

"June hasn't said anything about that," Maria said, her voice professional, though June thought she detected a tremor. "I need her here at the hospital. Things are always busy after the holidays, and June has already taken her time off."

"Maria?" June heard a man's voice shout. *Frank Chavez?* Then she heard something that sounded like a chair crashing to the floor, feet pounding, and men shouting. A shot rang out. She crouched between the toilet and the washbasin and tried to make herself small. But when she heard Maria scream "No!" she couldn't remain there. Throwing open the bathroom door, she took in the scene.

Frank Chavez and a uniformed man she'd never seen held Ray pinned face-down to the floor as they clasped handcuffs around his wrists. Maria sobbed quietly as she knelt beside another man, gently removing the shirt of his uniform to reveal a wounded shoulder, applying pressure with a towel as the blood soaked through, assuring him that he would live.

Ray turned his head toward her, and their eyes locked, before he was pulled to his feet and led away.

Epilogue

JUNE tied the sash of Maria's wedding gown—a traditional white satin and lace confection with modest neckline and capped sleeves—then arranged the folds of a long gossamer-thin veil over it. "Momma always said I tied a perfect bow," she drawled, smiling at her friend's reflection in the mirror. "I believe you are the most beautiful bride I've ever seen."

"Thank you, June," Maria said, turning to hug her, "and thank you for being here to help make this a perfect day."

"I wouldn't miss your wedding for anything, darlin.'" June meant this sincerely, although when she left Arizona six months ago, she wasn't sure she would ever have the courage to return. The stress of realizing how close she had come to being kidnapped, the horror of having her best friend's fiancée shot by her own lover on the same day she had lost her friend Jae to cancer—it had been almost too much to bear, and she feared being back in the desert would trigger the trauma. But so far, the joy of the occasion and the chance to be with her friends again outweighed any distress that she felt. Moving back to her roots, where she could drive to see her daughter in just over two hours, had been a good decision for her. She felt she was making great progress—with the help of an excellent therapist—in putting her life back together.

Savannah peeked her head around the door, which was slightly ajar. "Come on, Momma, the organist is playing, it's time for us to sit." She let out a little gasp when she saw Maria. "Oh my goodness," she said, "how beautiful…"

Frank, holding Margaret's hand, appeared behind Savannah. He pushed the door open further with his free hand, then stepped back, a look of admiration on his face. "*Hermanita,* you are stunning. Are you ready? I don't think we should make this good man wait a minute longer."

The vows, like the gown, were traditional. "I, Maria, take you, Tony, to be my husband, to have and to hold from this day forward, for better, for worse, for richer, for poorer, in sickness and in health, to love and to cherish…until death do us part."

Coming in 2026,
Second to Die,
next in the Saguaro series.

Acknowledgments

PUBLISHING a book requires attention to so many details, and involves so many people, that I will never again take a volume for granted.

I want to thank my writing partners, Ellen Fisher and Joel Johnson, for faithfully meeting me—virtually—three mornings a week over the nine months during which *A Murder at Rancho Manana* was written. A special word of thanks to my Chamonix writing sisters, and to author friends Nancy, Kathy, Christie, and Ginny—to name a few—for lending their experience and encouragement.

Cam Torrens, award-winning author of the Tyler Zahn mystery suspense series, was generous with his time—reading and re-reading my manuscript and providing valuable insights. John McFarlane, another beta reader and my favorite law enforcement officer, provided feedback on character development and plot. Of course my husband, Andy Kenney, always gets the first peek.

My editor, Eva Fox Mate, of Gemini Writer's Studio, provided excellent resources for perfecting the manuscript, then personally perfected it further.

Veronica Yager, director and founder of Journey Bound Publishing, and Cheryl Callighan, my dedicated contact on Veronica's team, put it all together in a package I feel proud to offer my readers.

I am surrounded by cheerleaders—friends and family members who ask me how my book is coming, and say they can't wait to read it. That's all the motivation I need.

Sherry Hester Kenney